Praise for Cindi Myers

"Myers's ability to portray true-to-life sympathetic characters will resonate most with readers of this captivating romance."
—*Publishers Weekly* on *Learning Curves*

"Delightful and delicious...Cindi Myers always satisfies!"
—*USA TODAY* bestselling author Julie Ortolon

"Charming. The protagonists' chemistry and Lucy's spunk keep this fluffy novel grounded."
—*Publishers Weekly* on *Life According to Lucy*

"The story is rife with insight and irony, and the characters are just plain fun."
—*Romantic Times BOOKclub* on *Detour Ahead*

"Ms. Myers will definitely keep readers sighing with delight."
—Writers Unlimited

Cindi Myers

Cindi Myers wrote her first short story at age eight and spent many a math class thereafter writing fiction instead of fractions. Her favorite childhood retreat was a tree house, where she would spend hours reading, and watching birds. As an adult, she continued this love of both birds and books. She became a journalist, and then a novelist. An avid skier, hiker, gardener and quilter, she lives in the Rocky Mountains with her husband, two spoiled dogs and a demanding parrot. She's the keeper of numerous bird feeders and avoids math whenever possible. *The Birdman's Daughter* is her twenty-second published novel.

→ CINDI MYERS ←

THE BIRDMAN'S DAUGHTER

THE BIRDMAN'S DAUGHTER

copyright © 2006 by Cynthia Myers

i s b n   0 3 7 3 8 8 0 8 8 X

TheNextNovel.com

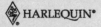 HARLEQUIN®

PRINTED IN U.S.A.

For Daddy

PROLOGUE

*There are joys which long to be ours. God sends
ten thousand truths, which come about us like birds
seeking inlet; but we are shut up to them, and so
they bring us nothing, but sit and sing awhile upon
the roof, and then fly away.*
—Henry Ward Beecher

For a man who'd spent his childhood on the arid plains of west Texas, the jungle was a place of magic. Martin Engel had hardly slept the night before, anxious to be on the trail again, completing his quest. He'd roused his companion on this trip, Allen Welch, from bed at 3:00 a.m. "We've got to be there before dawn," he'd reminded Welch. "We're going to have good luck today. I can feel it."

Martin's intuition was seldom wrong. Some people complained that he'd had more than his share of good luck in his pursuits, but Martin preferred to depend on hard work and experience. Over the years he'd taught himself everything there was to know about his quarry.

Still, there was something mystical about the hunt, a point in every search where he found himself locked in, putting himself on a different plane, trying to *think* like the ones he sought.

Martin was a birder. Not a backyard hobbyist or vacation afficionado. He was an acknowledged champion, a "big lister" who had seen more different kinds of birds than only a handful of people in the world.

Seven thousand, nine hundred and forty-eight. Today he was trying for seven thousand, nine hundred and fifty. On this trip he planned to clean up Brazil. When he got on the plane to head home to Texas, he would have seen every bird that existed in this country's jungles and plains. The promise of such an accomplishment made him tremble with excitement.

He and Welch were at the trailhead by 3:30. Welch slugged coffee from a thermos and stumbled over roots in the path, while Martin charged forward, eyes scanning the canopy overhead, binoculars ready. Even at this early hour, the air was thick and fetid around him, the ground beneath his feet spongy with decay. His ears filled with the whirring of insects. Insects meant birds.

He reviewed his quarry in his mind. The Pale-faced Antbird, *Skutchia borbae*, with its dark rufous head and black eye-patch; the Hoffman's Woodcreeper, *Dendrocolaptes hoffmannsi*, with its straight blackish bill and the brown to rufous-chestnut upperparts; and the

Brown-chested Barbet, *Capito brunneipectus*, with its distinctive chunky silhouette. They had haunted him for months now, taunting him with the blank lines beside their names on his list, lines where he would record the date, time and location of his sighting of them.

He'd seen the Pale-faced Antbird his first day out this trip. He and Welch had scarcely stepped onto the jungle path when it flashed by them, lured by the sounds of a Pale-faced Antbird call Martin had played on the tape deck strapped to his pack. The other two had been more wary. He'd hunted three days for them, scarcely noticing the sweat drenching his clothes or the hunger pangs in his belly or the cotton in his mouth.

Only two more names and he would have cleaned up Brazil. Only fifty more birds and he would have his eight thousand, within reach of the record as the most accomplished birder in the world. And he'd done it all on his own, while working and raising a family. No fancy paid guides to point out the birds for him. He'd taught himself to recognize them and tramped out to hunt on his own.

People talked about the ecstasy of drugs or spiritual quests. For him that feeling came when he spotted a new bird to add to his list. The flash of wing, a hint of color, the silhouette of a distinct form against the sky was like a glimpse of the divine. He, Martin Engel, unremarkable middle son in a large family of accomplished athletes and academics, had been singled out for this privilege. With each new sighting, his heart raced, his palms grew clammy, and his breath came in gasps. When he was certain of his quarry, he'd been known to shout and pump his fists. A new bird added to his list was the equivalent of a grand slam in the World Series. He'd done what few in the world had ever accomplished.

Sometimes guilt pricked at him—guilt over spending so much time away from his family. But more often than not, he didn't think about them. When he was out there, hunting, it was all about the birds and the numbers.

He'd awakened this morning with the sense that this would be the day he'd see the other two birds he needed. But as the morning dragged on, his certainty faded. The trees were filled with Variegated Antpittas, Fuscous and Boat-billed Flycatchers and White-throated Hummingbirds—all birds he'd seen before. As if to taunt him, a second Pale-faced Antbird darted across the path in front of them. But no sign of the Woodcreeper or the Barbet.

"We should stop and rest," Welch said, coming up behind Martin when he stopped to train his binoculars on a bird overhead. A Glittering-bellied Emerald, its iridescent blue and green feathers shimmering in a beam of sunlight.

"Just a little farther," Martin said, letting the binoculars hang loose around his neck again. "We're close."

"It's like a steam room out here." Welch wiped at his neck with a crumpled bandanna.

"Is it?" Martin hadn't noticed.

He'd known this feeling before, this sense that the bird he sought was nearby. He only had to look at the right location at the right moment and it would be his.

And that was how it was again. He turned his head slightly, prepared to argue with Welch, and he saw the flash of color in the trees. He froze and brought his binoculars up to his eye, his spirits soaring as he zeroed in on the distinctive straight black bill. "That's it!" he shouted, adrenaline surging through him. "I told you it was here."

But the last words came out muddled, and the next thing he knew, he was sinking to his knees in the thick forest muck, the world whirling around him, until he was staring up at a wavery patch of sky framed by leafy branches. Welch was saying something to him, something he couldn't hear. All he could think as he slipped into blackness was *Only one more bird to go....*

CHAPTER 1

*Life is good only when it is magical and
musical... You must hear the bird's song without
attempting to render it into nouns and verbs.*
—*Ralph Waldo Emerson, "Works and Days"*

When Karen MacBride first saw her father in the
hospital, she was struck by how much this man who had
spent his life pursuing birds had come to resemble one.
His head, round and covered with wispy gray hair,
reminded her of the head of a baby bird. His thin arms
beneath the hospital sheet folded up against his body
like wings. Years spent outdoors had weathered his face
until his nose jutted out like a beak, his eyes sunken in
hollows, watching her with the cautious interest of a
crow as she approached his bed.

"Hi, Dad." She offered a smile and lightly touched
his arm. "I've come home to take care of you for a
while." After sixteen years away from Texas, she'd
flown from her home in Denver this morning to help
with her father for a few weeks.

That she'd agreed to do so surprised her. Martin Engel was not a man who either offered or inspired devotion from his family. He had been the remote authority figure of Karen's childhood, the distracted voice on the other end of the line during infrequent phone calls during her adult years, the polite, preoccupied host during scattered visits home. For as long as she could remember, conversations with her father had had a disjointed quality, as if all the time he was talking to her, he was thinking of the call of the Egyptian Goose, or a reputed sighting of a rare Hutton's Shearwater.

Which of course, he was. So what kind of communication could she expect from him now that he couldn't talk at all? Maybe she'd agreed to return to Texas in order to find out.

He nodded to show he understood her now, and made a guttural noise in his throat, like the complaining of a jay.

"The doctors say there's a chance he will talk again." Karen's mother, Sara, spoke from her post at the end of the bed. "A speech therapist will come once a week to work with him, and the occupational therapist twice a week. Plus there's an aide every weekday to help with bathing and things like that."

Karen swallowed hard, resisting the urge to turn and run, all the way back to Colorado. A voice in her head whispered, *It's not too late to get out of this, you know*.

She ignored the voice and nodded, smile still firmly

fixed in place. "The caseworker gave me the schedule. And Del said he got the house in order."

"He built a ramp for the wheelchair and put hand-rails in the shower and things." Sara folded her arms over her stomach, still looking grim. "Thank God you agreed to come down and stay with him. Three days with him here has been enough to wear me out."

"Mom!" Karen nodded to her dad.

"I know he can hear me." Sara swatted at her former husband's leg. "I'm sure it hasn't been any more pleasant for him than it has been for me." Sara and Martin Engel had divorced some twenty years before, but they still lived in the same town and maintained a polite, if distant, relationship.

A large male nurse's aide filled the doorway of the room. "Mr. Engel, I'm here to help you get dressed so you can go home."

"Karen and I will go get a cup of coffee." Sara took her daughter by the arm and pulled her down the hallway.

"You looked white as a ghost back there," Sara said as they headed toward the cafeteria. "You aren't going to get all weak and weepy on me, are you?"

Karen took a deep breath and shook her head. "No." It had been a shock, seeing Dad like that. But she was okay now. She could do this.

"Good. Because he's not worth shedding any tears over."

Karen said nothing. She knew for a fact her mother

had cried buckets of tears over Martin at one time. "What happened, exactly?" she said. "I understand he's had a stroke, but how?"

"He was in Brazil, hunting the Pale-faced Antbird, the Hoffman's Woodcreeper and the Brown-chested Barbet." Sara rattled off the names of the exotic birds without hesitation. Living with a man devoted to birding required learning to speak the language in order to have much communication from him at all. She glanced over the top of her bifocals at her daughter. "If he found those three, he'd have 'cleaned up' Brazil, so of course he was adamant it be done as soon as possible."

"He only needed three birds to have seen every bird in Brazil?" Karen marveled at this. "How many is that?"

"Seven thousand, nine hundred and something?" Sara shook her head. "I'm not sure. It changes all the time anyway. But I do know he's getting close to eight thousand. When he passed seven thousand, seven hundred and fifty, he became positively fanatical about topping eight thousand before he got too old to travel."

Ever since Karen could remember, her father's life—and thus the life of his family—had revolved around adding birds to the list. By the time she was six, Karen could name over a hundred different types of birds. She rattled off genus species names the way other children talked about favorite cartoon characters. Instead of commercial jingles, birdcalls stuck in her head, and played over and over again. To this day, when she heard an Olive-sided Flycatcher, she could remember the spring morning when she'd first identified it on her own, and been lavished with praise by her too-often-distracted father.

"He'd just spotted the Woodcreeper when he keeled over right there in the jungle." Sara continued her story. "Allen Welch was with him, and he's the one who called me. He apologized, but said he had no idea who else to contact."

Karen shook her head, amazed. "How did you ever get him home?"

"The insurance paid for an air ambulance. All those years with Mobil Oil were worth something after all." Martin had spent his entire career as a petroleum engineer with Mobil Oil Company. He always told people he kept the job for the benefits. They assumed he meant health insurance and a pension, but his family knew the chief benefit for him was the opportunity to travel all over the world, adding birds to his list.

They reached the cafeteria. "I'll get the coffee, you sit," Sara said, and headed for the coffee machine.

Karen sank into a molded plastic chair and checked her watch. Eleven in the morning here in Texas. Only ten in Colorado. Tom and Matt would be at a job site by now and Casey was in math class—she hoped.

"Here you go." Her mother set a cardboard cup in front of her and settled into the chair across the table. "How are Tom and the boys?"

"They're fine. This is always a busy time of year for us, of course, but Matt's been a terrific help, and we've hired some new workers." Tom and Karen owned Blue Spruce Landscaping. This past year, their oldest son, Matt, had begun working for them full-time. "Did I tell you Matt's signed up for classes at Red Rocks Community College this fall? He wants to study landscaping."

"And he'll be great at it, I'm sure." She sipped her coffee. "What about Casey? What's he up to these days?"

Karen's stomach tightened as she thought of her youngest son. "Oh, you know Casey. Charming and sweet and completely unmotivated." She made a face. "He's failing two classes this semester. I'm beginning to wonder if I'll ever get him out of high school."

"He takes after his uncle Del." Sara's smile was fond, but her words made Karen shudder.

"The world doesn't need two Dels," she said. Her younger brother was a handsome, glib, womanizing con man. When he wasn't sponging off her parents, he was making a play for some woman—usually one young enough to be his daughter. "Are he and Sheila still together?" Sheila was Del's third wife, the one who'd put up with him the longest.

"No, they've split up." Sara shrugged. "No surprise there. She never let the boy have any peace. Talk about a shrew."

"I'd be a shrew, too, if my husband couldn't keep his pants zipped or his bank account from being overdrawn."

"Now, your brother has a good heart. People—especially women—always take advantage of him."

No, Del had a black heart, and he was an expert at taking advantage of others. But Karen knew it was no use arguing with her mother. "If Del's so good, maybe *he* should be the one looking after Dad," she said.

Her mother frowned at her. "You know your father and Del don't get along. Besides, for all his good qualities, Del isn't the most responsible man in the world."

Any other time, Karen might have laughed. Saying her brother wasn't responsible was like saying the Rocky Mountains were steep.

She checked her watch again. Eleven-twenty. At home she'd be making the last calls on her morning's to-do list.

Here, there was no to-do list, just this sense of too much to handle. Too many hours where she didn't know what lay ahead. Too many things she had no control over. "Do you think he's ready yet?" she asked.

Her mother stood. "He probably is. I'll help you get him in the car. Del said he'd meet you at the house to help get him inside, but after that, you're on your own."

"Right." After all, she was Karen, the oldest daughter. The dependable one.

The one with *sucker* written right across her forehead.

Of course Del was nowhere in sight when Karen pulled her father's Jeep Cherokee up to the new wheel-

chair ramp in front of his house. She got out of the car
and took a few steps toward the mobile home parked
just across the fence, but Del's truck wasn't under the
carport and there was no sign that anyone was home.

Anger gnawing a hole in her gut, she went around
to the back of the Jeep and took out the wheelchair her
mother had rented from the hospital pharmacy. After
five minutes of struggling in the already oppressive May
heat, she figured out how to set it up, and wheeled it
around to the passenger side of the vehicle.

"Okay, Dad, you're going to have to help me with
this," she said, watching his eyes to make sure he understood.

He nodded and grunted again, and made a move
toward the chair.

"Wait, let me unbuckle your seat belt. Okay, put
your hand on my shoulder. Wait, I'm not ready…well,
all right. Here. Wait—"

Martin half fell and was half dragged into the chair.
Sweat trickled down Karen's back and pooled at the
base of her spine. She studied the wheelchair ramp her
brother had built out of plywood. As usual, he'd done
a half-ass job. The thing was built like a skateboard
ramp, much too steep.

In the end, she had to drag the chair up the ramp
backwards, grappling for purchase on the slick plywood
surface, cursing her brother under her breath the whole
way. At the top, she sagged against the front door and

dug in her purse for the key. A bird sang from the top of the pine tree beside the house.

She felt a tug on her shirt and looked over to find her father staring intently at the tree. "Northern Cardinal," she identified the bird.

He nodded, satisfied, apparently, that she hadn't forgotten everything he'd taught her.

Inside, the air-conditioning hit them with a welcome blast of cold. Karen pushed the wheelchair through the living room, past the nubby plaid sofa that had sat in the same spot against the wall for the past thirty years, and the big-screen TV that was a much newer addition. She started to turn toward her father's bedroom, but he tugged at her again, and indicated he wanted to go in the opposite direction.

"Do you want to go to your study?" she asked, dismayed.

He nodded.

"Maybe you should rest first. Or the two of us could visit some. I could make lunch...."

He shook his head, and made a stabbing motion with his right hand toward the study.

She reluctantly turned the chair toward the back bedroom that none of them had been allowed to enter without permission when she was a child.

The room was paneled in dark wood, most of the floor space taken up by a scarred wooden desk topped by a sleek black computer tower and flat-screen monitor. Karen shoved the leather desk chair aside and wheeled her father's chair into the kneehole. Before he'd come to a halt, he'd reached out with his right hand and hit the button to turn the computer on.

She backed away, taking the opportunity to study the room. Except for the newer computer, things hadn't changed much since her last visit, almost a year ago. A yellowing map filled one wall, colored pins marking the countries where her father had traveled and listed birds. Behind the desk, floor-to-ceiling shelves were filled with her father's collection of birding reference books, checklists and the notebooks in which he recorded the sightings made on each expedition.

The wall to the left of the desk was almost completely filled with a large picture window that afforded a view of the pond at the back of his property. From his seat at the desk, Martin could look up and see the Cattle Egrets, Black-necked Stilts, Least Terns and other birds that came to drink.

On the wall opposite the desk he had framed his awards. Pride of place was given to a citation from the *Guinness Book of World Records*, in 1998, when they recognized him as the first person to see at least one species of each of the world's one hundred and fifty-nine bird families in a single year. Around it were ranged lesser honors from the various birding societies to which he belonged.

She looked at her father again. He was bent over the

computer, his right hand gripping the mouse like an eagle's talon wrapped around a stone. "I'll fix us some lunch, okay?"

He said nothing, gaze riveted to the screen.

While Karen was making a sandwich in the kitchen, the back door opened to admit her brother. "Hey, sis," he said, wrapping his arms around her in a hug.

She gave in to the hug for two seconds, welcoming her brother's strength, and the idea that she could lean on him if she needed to. But of course, that was merely an illusion. She shrugged out of his grasp and continued slathering mayonnaise on a slice of bread. "You were supposed to be here to help get Dad in the house."

"I didn't know you were going to show up so soon. I ran out to get a few groceries." He pulled a six-pack of beer from the bag and broke off a can.

"You thought beer was appropriate for a man who just got out of the hospital?"

"I know I sure as hell would want one." He sat down and stretched his legs out in front of him. "Make me one of them sandwiches, will you?"

"Make your own." She dropped the knife in the mayonnaise jar, picked up the glass of nutritional supplement that was her father's meal, and went to the study.

When she returned to the kitchen, Del was still there. He was eating a sandwich, drinking a second beer. The jar of mayonnaise and loaf of bread still sat, open, on the counter. "I'm not your maid," she snapped. "Clean up after yourself."

"I see Colorado hasn't improved your disposition any." He nodded toward the study. "How's the old man?"

"Okay, considering. He can't talk yet, and he can't use his left side much at all, but his right side is okay."

"So how long are you staying?"

"A few weeks. Maybe a couple of months." She wiped crumbs from the counter and twisted the bread wrapper shut, her hands moving of their own accord. Efficient. Busy. "Just until he can look after himself again."

"You think he'll be able to do that?"

His skepticism rankled. "Of course he will. There will be therapists working with him almost every day."

"Better you than me." He crushed the beer can in his palm. "Spending that much time with him would drive me batty inside of a week."

She turned, her back pressed to the counter, and fixed her brother with a stern look. "You're going to have to do your part, Del. I can't do this all by myself."

"What about all those therapists?" He stood. "I'll send Mary Elisabeth over. She likes everybody."

"Who's Mary Elisabeth?"

"This girl I'm seeing."

That figured. The divorce papers for wife number three weren't even signed and he had a new female following after him. "How old is Mary Elisabeth?"

"Old enough." He grinned. "Younger than you. Prettier, too."

He left, and she sank into a chair. She'd hoped that at forty-one years old, she'd know better than to let her brother needle her that way. And that at thirty-nine, he'd be mature enough not to go out of his way to push her buttons.

But of course, anyone who thought that would be wrong. Less than an hour in the house she'd grown up in and she'd slipped into the old roles so easily—dutiful daughter, aggravated older sister.

She heard a hammering sound and realized it was her father, summoning her. She jumped up and went to him. He'd managed to type a message on the screen
I'm ready for bed.

She wheeled him to his bedroom. Some time ago he'd replaced the king-size bed he'd shared with her mother with a double, using the extra space to install a spotting scope on a stand, aimed at the trees outside the window. Nearby sat a tape recorder and a stack of birdcall tapes, along with half a dozen field guides.

She reached to unbutton his shirt and he pushed her away, his right arm surprisingly strong. She frowned at him. "Let me help you, Dad. It's the reason I came all this way. I *want* to help you."

Their eyes meet, his watery and pale, with only a hint of their former keenness. Her breath caught as the realization hit her that he was an old man. Aged.

Infirm. Words she had never, ever associated with her strong, proud father. The idea unnerved her.

He looked away from her, shoulders slumped, and let her wrestle him out of his clothes and into pajamas. He got into bed and let her arrange his legs under the covers and tuck him in. Then he turned his back on her. She was dismissed.

She went into the living room and lay down on the sofa. The clock on the shelf across the room showed 1:35. She felt like a prisoner on the first day of a long sentence.

A sentence she'd volunteered for, she reminded herself. Though God knew why. Maybe she'd indulged a fantasy of father-daughter bonding, of a dad so grateful for his daughter's assistance that he'd finally open up to her. Or that he'd forget about birds for a while and nurture a relationship with her.

She might as well have wished for wings and the ability to fly.

CHAPTER 2

You must have the bird in your heart before you
can find it in the bush.
—*John Burroughs,* Birds and Bees, Sharp Eyes
and Other Papers

When Karen woke the next morning, she stared up at the familiar-yet-not-quite-right ceiling, then rolled over, reaching for Tom. But of course, he wasn't here. She sat up and looked around the bedroom she'd occupied as a girl. A line of neon-haired Troll dolls leered back at her from the bookshelves beside the window.

The clock showed 7:25. She lay on her back, sleep still pulling at her. She told herself she should get up and check on her father. The occupational therapist was coming this morning and the nurse's aide was due after lunch. Today would set the tone for the rest of her days here, so she needed to get off on the right foot. Still she lingered under the comfort of the covers.

When she did finally force herself into a sitting

position, she reached for the phone. Tom would be up by now, getting breakfast for himself and the boys.

"Hello?" He answered on the third ring.

"Hi, honey. Good morning."

"Good morning. How's it going?"

"Okay, so far. Dad's not as helpless as I thought. He can't talk, but he can type with his right hand on the computer, and he tries to help me move him in and out of his chair, though sometimes that's more trouble than if he sat still. The therapist is coming today to start working with him, so I'm hoping for good progress."

"That's good. Don't try to do too much by yourself, though. Get some help."

"I saw Del yesterday. I told him he'd have to help me and he volunteered his girlfriend-du-jour."

Tom laughed and she heard the scrape of a spatula against a pan. He was probably making eggs. "How's it going there?" she asked.

"Hectic, as usual. We're starting that big job out at Adventist Hospital today, and we've still got ten houses left to do in that new development out near the airport."

Guilt squeezed her at the thought of all the paperwork those jobs would entail in the coming weeks. She was the one who kept the office running smoothly, not to mention their household. "Maybe you should hire some temporary help in the office," she said. "Just until I get back."

"Maybe. But I don't trust a stranger the way I trust you. Besides, you'll be back soon."

Not soon enough to suit her. In nearly twenty-three years of marriage, they'd never been apart more than a night or two. The thought of weeks without him, away from her familiar routine, made her want to crawl back in bed and pull up the covers until this was all over. "How are the boys?"

"Matt's doing great. He's running a crew for me on those subdivision jobs."

"And Casey?" She held her breath, waiting for news of her problem youngest child.

"I got a call from the school counselor last night. He's going to fail his freshman year of high school unless he can pull off a miracle on his final exams. And he's decided he doesn't want to work for me this summer."

There was no mistaking the edge in Tom's voice. He took this kind of thing personally, though she doubted Casey meant it that way. "What does he want to do?"

"Apparently nothing."

"Let me talk to him."

She heard him call for Casey, and then her youngest son was on the phone, as cheerful as if he'd been awake for hours, instead of only a few minutes. "Hey, Mom, how are you? I thought about you last night. Justin and I went to see this really cool band. They write all their own songs and stuff. You would have really liked them."

It would have been easier to come down hard on Casey if he were surly and uncommunicative, but he had always been a sunny child. She reminded herself it was her job as a mother to try to balance out some of that sunniness with reality. "Dad tells me the school counselor called him last night."

"It's all such a crock," he said. "All they do is teach these tests. The teachers don't care if we learn anything useful or not. Why should I even bother?"

"You should bother because a high school diploma is a requirement for even the most entry-level jobs these days, and Mom and Dad aren't going to be around to support you forever."

"You don't have to worry about me, Mom. I'll be okay."

Okay doing what? she wanted to ask, but didn't dare. The last time she'd hazarded this question, he'd shared his elaborate plan to become a championship surfer in Hawaii—despite the fact that he'd never been on a surfboard before.

"What are you going to do this summer?" she asked instead. He had only one more week of school before vacation.

"I thought maybe I'd just, you know, hang out."

He was fast becoming an expert at *hanging out*. "Your dad could really use your help. Without me there he's having to do more of the office work."

"Matt's helping him. A friend of mine has a job lifeguarding at the city pool. He thinks he can get me on there. That would be a cool job."

Any job was better than no job, she supposed. "All right, if you get the job, I'll talk to your dad."

"When are you coming home?"

The plaintive tone in his voice cut deep. "I don't know. In a few weeks. By the end of the summer, for sure." Her original plan for a short visit seemed unrealistic now that she'd seen her father and realized the extent of his disability.

"How's Grandpa?"

"He's okay. The stroke paralyzed his left side, though with therapy, he should be able to get back to almost normal." She hoped.

"That's good. Tell him I said hi. Dad wants to talk to you again."

Tom got back on the line. "He says he's going to get a job lifeguarding at the city pool," she said. "Maybe it would be a good thing for him to work for someone else for a summer."

"Yeah, then he'd find out how good he's got it now." He shifted the phone and called goodbye to the boys as they left for school and work, then returned to their conversation. "What did you tell Casey when he asked how long you'd be gone?"

"I told him I'll be home by the end of the summer, at the latest." She didn't know if she'd last that long, but she'd made a commitment and couldn't back out now.

"I don't know how we're going to do without you here for that long. I was thinking it would only be a few weeks."

She took a deep breath, fighting against the tension that tightened around her chest like a steel band. "I know I said that, but now that I'm here, I can see that was unrealistic. He's going to need more time to get back on his feet."

"Then your mother and brother should pitch in to help. They live right there and neither one of them has a family."

"They won't help. Del hardly spent five minutes here yesterday."

"What about a nursing home? Or a rehab facility? His insurance would probably even pay for part of it." Tom was in problem solving mode now. For him, everything had a simple answer. But there was nothing simple about her relationship with her father.

"It would kill him to be in a place like that. To have strangers taking care of him. You know how he is about his privacy. His dignity."

"I know he's never gone out of his way to do anything for you. And we need you here." The no-nonsense tone she admired when Tom dealt with vendors and difficult customers wasn't as welcome when it was aimed at her.

"I know you do," she said, struggling to keep her temper. She'd been away from home scarcely twenty-four hours and he was already complaining. She'd wanted sympathy from him. Support. Not a lecture. "Right now, Dad needs me more."

"What are you going to do if your father doesn't recover enough to look after himself again?" Tom asked.

"I don't know." Having him come live with them in Denver was out of the question. The doctor had already told her his lungs couldn't handle the altitude. She sighed. "If Dad doesn't improve by the end of the summer, we'll probably have to put him in a nursing home. But give me this summer to try to help him, please."

"I'm sorry." His voice softened. "I don't mean to pressure you. I just…it's hard to think about dealing with the business and the boys without you. Casey's not the only one in this house who didn't realize how good he's got it."

She laughed, as much from relief as mirth. "You keep thinking like that. And see when you can get away to come see me."

"I'll do that."

They said their goodbyes, then she dressed and made her bed, and went to get her father ready for his first therapy appointment.

What she hadn't been able to say to Tom was that she needed to stay here right now as much for herself as for her father. She needed to see if being forced together like this, they could somehow find the closeness that had always eluded them before.

* * *

That afternoon, Casey lay on his bed and tossed a minibasketball at the hoop on the back of the bedroom door. If he aimed it just right, the ball would soar through the hoop, bounce off the door and sail back to him, so that he could retrieve it and start over without changing positions.

Matt was in the shower in the bathroom next to the bedroom they shared. Casey could hear the water pounding against the tile wall, and smell the herbal shampoo Matt liked. He was getting ready to go on a date with his girlfriend, Audra. Were they going to have sex? Casey knew they'd done it because he'd caught Matt hiding a box of condoms in the back of his desk drawer, where he thought Mom wouldn't find them. Casey had given him a hard time about it. "You're nineteen, for Christ's sake," he'd said, while his older brother's face turned the color of a ripe tomato. "You shouldn't have to hide something like that."

Matt had shoved the box back in the drawer. "Right. Mom would have a cow if she knew."

"Mom's always having cows. She'll get over it."

He smiled and tossed the ball again, remembering the exchange. The trick to handling Mom was to smile and nod and let her go on for a while, then give her a hug or a kiss and continue as you always had. She was really pretty easy to handle once you knew the secret.

She'd sounded all worried and sad on the phone this morning. Maybe she was upset about Grandpa. That would be pretty rough, seeing your dad in the hospital, all helpless and old. That had probably freaked her out. Mom pretended to be all tough sometimes, but she was still a girl.

He caught the basketball on the rebound and launched it again. What would it be like to have a stroke? Mom had said Grandpa couldn't use his left side. Casey lay back and stiffened his left arm and leg, pretending they were useless. He imagined trying to walk, dragging his paralyzed leg behind him. If you tried to eat, would you get food all over yourself?

He relaxed and let his mind drift to other topics. Mom had said she'd talk to Dad about the lifeguard job. That was cool. He knew he was a disappointment to his dad, who wanted him to be more like Matt. Matt was the perfect son. He was going to college and would take over the business someday. Cool, if that's what he wanted, but couldn't they see Casey didn't want anything like that?

Trouble was, he wasn't sure what he wanted. Still, he was only sixteen. He had plenty of time to figure it out. Whatever he ended up doing, it wasn't going to require going to school for years and years. Maybe he'd be a musician or an artist. Or he'd invent something fantastic that would make him tons of money.

Maybe he'd be a writer. He'd like that. For as long

as he could remember he'd kept notebooks full of his writing—stories, poems, even songs.

Matt came out of the bathroom and threw a wet towel at him. "I need to borrow your hair gel," he said.

"For a dollar."

"What?" Matt glared at him.

"You can borrow my hair gel for a dollar."

"You're crazy." Matt turned away.

Casey didn't argue. The problem with Matt was that he carried the honest, upstanding young man thing too far. If it had been Casey, he would have used his brother's gel without asking and chances were, Matt never even would have noticed.

"Here, loser." Matt turned back and tossed a dollar bill toward the bed.

Casey reached out and caught it, smiling to himself. He knew big bro would pay up. He probably hadn't even thought long about not doing it.

Mentally, he added the dollar to the stash in his backpack. He had almost two hundred dollars now. Not bad for a guy without a job. He made money other ways, like writing love notes to girls for their boyfriends, or blackmailing the jocks who smoked out behind the gym. Dangerous work, but so far he'd managed to charm his way out of harm.

It was a gift, this ability to smile and talk his way out of tricky situations. A man with a gift like that could go far, no doubt.

"So are you going to work with us this summer?" Matt studied Casey in the dresser mirror as he rubbed gel through his hair.

"No, I'm going to get a job as a lifeguard at the city pool."

"You can't make a career out of being a lifeguard."

"Why not, if I want to?"

"For one thing, what'll you do in the winter, when the pool closes?"

"Maybe I'll move to Florida, or California, where the pools never close."

"You are such a loser." Matt pulled a shirt over his head, sneered at his brother one last time, then left.

Casey sighed and lay back on the bed again. Why did people think if you weren't just like them, you had to be wrong?

He thought about Mom again. Had she sounded so sad on the phone because she was worried about him? He'd tried to tell her she had nothing to worry about, but she probably couldn't help it. Worrying was a mom thing, like the way she told them, every time they left the house, "Be careful."

"No, tonight I think I'll be reckless," he always answered. She pretended not to think that was funny, but her eyes told him she was laughing on the inside.

He missed her. She'd sounded like she missed them, too. He sat up, put the dollar in his pocket, and decided he'd take a walk downtown, to see what was going on.

* * *

While Martin worked with the occupational thera-pist, an energetic young woman named Lola, Karen took inventory of the refrigerator and pantry and made a shopping list. When the nurse's aide came this after-noon, Karen could slip out to buy groceries and refill Dad's medications.

She was disposing of half a dozen petrified packages of frozen food in the outside trash can when a red minivan pulled into the driveway. As she waited with her hand on the garbage can lid, a plump blonde in pink capris and a pink-and-white striped sleeveless shirt slid from the driver's seat. The blonde propped her sun-glasses on top of her head and waved.

Karen broke into a run, laughing as she embraced Tammy Collins Wainwright. "Look at you, girl!" Tammy drew back and looked Karen up and down. "I guess living up there in the mountains and working at that landscape business is keeping you young and trim."

"Denver isn't really in the mountains, but I guess it does agree with me. And what about you? You look great." Except for a few lines on her forehead and around her eyes, Tammy hadn't changed much since their days behind the wheel in driver's ed class at Tipton Senior High School. The two girls had been pretty much inseparable after meeting in that class. They'd worked behind the counter together at the Dinky Dairy, and had double-dated whenever possible.

Tammy had been the matron of honor in Karen's wedding, having already married her high school sweetheart, Brady Wainwright. While Karen had moved to Austin and later Colorado, Tammy had stayed in town to raise four children; her youngest, April, was ten.

Tammy's smile faded. "I'm so sorry about your dad," she said. "It must be just awful for you."

Karen nodded, not quite sure how to respond. It was much more terrible for her father, after all. And it wasn't as if he'd died.

Or was Tammy referring to the fact that Karen had left everything she knew and loved to come take care of a man she wasn't even sure liked her?

"I brought a cake." Tammy reached into the van and pulled out a yellow-and-white Tupperware Cake Taker. "I remember how Mr. Martin had a real sweet tooth."

"And his daughter inherited it." Karen took the cake carrier from Tammy and walked beside her toward the house. "Did you make this yourself?" She couldn't remember the last time she'd made a cake.

"Me and Betty Crocker." Tammy threw her head back and let out peals of laughter.

Lola met them at the door, her "bag of tricks," as she called her therapy equipment, in hand. "He did very well for his first day," she said. "He's worn out, though. I imagine he'll sleep for a couple of hours or so. Just let him be and feed him when he wakes up. And I'll see you Thursday."

Karen thanked her, then led the way through the house to the screened back porch. This side of the house was shady, and two ceiling fans overhead stirred the slightly cool air. "Do you mind if we sit out here and visit?" she asked. "That way we won't disturb Dad."

"That would be great." Tammy settled in one of the cushioned patio chairs. "I wouldn't say no to a glass of iced tea."

"Coming right up. And I thought maybe we'd try this cake with it."

"I shouldn't, but I will."

Karen returned a few minutes later with two glasses of iced tea and two plates with generous slices of the lemon cake. "I already stole a bite," she said as she sat in the chair across from her friend. "It's delicious."

"Thank you." Tammy took a bite and moaned. "Ooooh, that *is* good, isn't it?"

"So tell me what you've been up to," Karen said. "How are Brady and the kids?"

"They're doing great. April is going into fifth grade in the fall. Brady's still racing. Our twenty-third wedding anniversary is next month and we're going to San Antonio for the weekend."

"That's great. Congratulations."

"I'm pretty excited. I can't remember the last time we went anywhere without the kids. Which is why I shouldn't be eating this cake." She pushed her empty plate away. "I want to still be able to fit into the new clothes I bought for the trip."

"Sounds like fun."

"Your twenty-third is coming up soon, isn't it?"

Karen nodded. "This fall. I can't believe it's been that long." It seemed like only yesterday she'd been working as a receptionist at the new hospital and Tom had been hired to do the landscaping work. He caused quite a stir among all the young women when he took off his shirt to plant a row of shrubs along the front drive. They'd all wasted countless hours admiring his bronzed muscles and tight blue jeans. When he'd asked Karen to go out with him, she'd been the envy of her coworkers.

"We're thinking about renewing our vows for our twenty-fifth. You and Tom should think about that. You never had a big wedding. This would be your chance."

Karen and Tom had eloped. They'd gone to Vegas for the weekend and been married at a chapel there. It had been very sweet and romantic, though at times she regretted not having the big church wedding with the long white dress, et cetera. She pressed the back of her fork into the last of the cake crumbs. "Did I ever tell you the real reason we eloped?" she asked.

Tammy's eyes widened. "Were you pregnant?"

She laughed. "No. It was because I was afraid my father wouldn't show up for the wedding and I wanted to save myself that humiliation."

"Oh, honey!" Tammy leaned over and squeezed

Karen's hand. "Of course he would have shown up for your wedding."

She shook her head. "He wasn't there for my high school graduation. He was in the Galapagos, bird-watching. When Matt was born, he was in Alaska, and when I had Casey, he was in Guatemala."

"But surely your wedding…"

"I didn't want to risk it."

Tammy sat back and assumed an upbeat tone once more. "Well, it doesn't matter how you got married. The point is, it took. Not many couples can say that these days."

She nodded. The fact that she and Tom had stayed together all these years was pretty amazing, considering they'd known each other all of three months when they decided to tie the knot. She had been only eighteen, trying to decide what to do with her future. She'd liked Tom well enough, but when he'd told her he planned to move to Austin at the end of the summer—over two hundred miles away from Tipton—she'd decided to throw in her lot with him.

She'd latched on to him as her ticket out of town, but stuck with him because he'd showed her a kind of love she'd never known before. Now he was the rock who supported her.

"So how is the birdman?" Tammy asked, using the name the townspeople had given Karen's father long ago.

"Cantankerous as ever." Karen sipped her iced tea,

then cradled the glass between her palms, letting the cold seep into her skin. "That's good, I guess. He's a fighter. He'll fight his way back from this, too."

"They did an article on him in the paper last year. Said he was one of the top ten bird-watchers in the whole world."

Her mother had sent her a copy of the article. "He's getting close to eight thousand birds on his list now."

"Goodness. I can't imagine seeing that many different birds."

"It's taken a long time." More to the point, listing birds had taken *all* his time, to the exclusion of almost everything else.

The doorbell sounded and both women jumped up. "That's probably the nurse's aide," Karen said. "The county is sending one every day to help with bathing and things like that."

"That's good. That'll help you." Tammy sighed and stood. "I'd better go. Jamie has a Little League game tonight, and April has piano practice. Somewhere in there I've got to figure out what to fix for supper."

"Thanks for the cake. And thanks for stopping by. It was good to see you."

They hugged, then walked arm-in-arm to the door. "If you need anything, you just holler," Tammy said. "And when you can get someone else to sit with Mr. Martin for a while, you come out and have dinner with us. Brady and the kids would love to see you."

"I'll do that." Karen let Tammy out and the aide in, then returned to her grocery list. Maybe staying here wasn't going to be such a hard thing, after all. She did have friends here, and this was a chance for her to get to know her father better, while he was forced to sit still.

It was a second chance for them, and how many people got second chances these days?

CHAPTER 3

Even the little sparrow, which flits about by the
roadside, can laugh at us with his impudent little
chirp, as he flies up out of reach to the topmost
branch of a tree.
—Arabella B. Buckley, The Fairy-Land of Science

Casey had never ridden a Greyhound bus before, but
it was pretty much the way he'd imagined: tall-backed,
plastic-covered seats filled with people who all looked
a little down on their luck. They wore old clothes and
carried shopping bags stuffed with packages and groceries and more old clothes. They were brown and black
and white, mostly young, but some old. The woman in
front of him had three little brown-haired, brown-eyed
boys who kept turning around in their seats to look at
him. Their mother would scold them in Spanish and
they would face forward again, only to look back in a
few minutes, unable to keep from staring at the white
kid all alone on the bus.

At first he'd only intended to see how much it would

cost to get from Denver to Tipton, Texas. But when he saw it was only a hundred and thirty dollars and there was a bus leaving in thirty minutes, he'd decided to buy the ticket and go. Mom had sounded so sad and worried on the phone. She was down there all alone with her sick father and nobody to help her, really. He could cheer her up and help, too.

The main thing about traveling on a bus was that it was boring. He spent a lot of time listening to CDs on his portable player and staring out the window. Not that there was much to see—the bus stayed on the interstate, mainly, cruising past fields and billboards and the occasional junkyard or strip of cheap houses. He made faces at the little boys in front of him, until their mother turned around and said something to him in Spanish. He didn't understand it, but from her tone it sounded as if she was cussing him out or something.

After that, he slept for a while. When he woke up, it was dark, and the bus was stopped at a station. "Where are we?" he asked the man in the seat behind him.

"Salina, Kansas," he said. "Dinner break."

At the mention of dinner, Casey's stomach rumbled. The driver wasn't anywhere in sight, so he figured that meant they were stopped for a while. He pulled himself up out of his seat and ambled down the aisle, in search of a diner or McDonald's or someplace to get something to eat.

The bus station was next to a Taco Bell. Casey

bought three burritos and a large Coke and ate at a little table outside. He thought he recognized a couple of other people from his bus, but they didn't say anything. They all looked tired or worried. He decided people who traveled by bus weren't doing it because they wanted adventure or a vacation, but because it was the cheapest way to get to where they needed to be.

When he got back on the bus, the seat he'd been sitting in was occupied by a thin guy with a shaved head. He had red-rimmed brown eyes that moved constantly. He looked at Casey, then away, then back again. Casey tried to ignore him, and searched for another seat, but the bus was full.

So he gingerly lowered himself into the seat next to the young man. "Hey," he said by way of greeting.

The guy didn't say anything. He just stared. He was skinny—so skinny his bones stuck out at his wrists and elbows and knees, like knobs on a tree limb. His plaid shirt and khaki pants still had creases in them from where they'd been folded in the package, and he wore tennis shoes without laces, the kind skateboarders used to wear five or six years ago.

The bus jerked forward and Casey folded his arms across his chest and slumped in his seat. It was going to be harder to sleep without the window to lean against, but he guessed he could manage it. Sleeping made the time pass faster, and he had the whole rest of the night and another day before they reached Tipton.

"What's your name?"

His seatmate's question startled him from a sound sleep. He opened his eyes and blinked in the darkness. The only light was the faint green glow from the dashboard far ahead, and the headlights of passing cars. He looked at the man next to him. "My name's Casey. What's yours?"

"My name's Denton. Denton Carver."

"Casey MacBride." Casey offered his hand and the man took it. His grip was hard, his palm heavily calloused. For someone so skinny, he was really strong.

"Where you goin'?" Denton asked.

"To Tipton, Texas. My mom's there, looking after my Grandpa, who's sick."

"That's too bad." Denton didn't look all that sorry, though.

"Where are you going?" Casey asked.

"Not sure, yet. Thought I'd get off in Houston and look around. I used to know some people there."

"So you're just, like, taking a vacation?" Maybe he'd been wrong about the people on the bus.

"You might say that." Denton grinned, showing yellow teeth. "I just got out of prison."

Casey went still. He told himself not to freak out or anything. He kept his expression casual. "I guess you're glad to be out, huh?"

Denton laughed, a loud bark that caused people around them to stir and look back. "I'm glad to be shed of that place, all right," he said.

Casey wondered what he'd been in prison for, but knew enough not to ask. He settled back in the seat and crossed his arms again. "Good luck in Houston," he said.

He closed his eyes, figuring Denton would get the message, but apparently once the skinny man had decided to talk, he wasn't interested in stopping. "I used to have a girlfriend in Houston. Her name was Thomasina. Kind of a weird name for a girl, but she was named after her daddy, Thomas. She was a big, tall girl, and she could hit like a man. She worked at this little store her daddy owned and once these two dudes tried to rob the place. She punched one guy in the nose and hit the other one upside the head with a can of green beans. He tried to run and she just wound up and threw that can at him. Knocked him out cold."

Casey stopped pretending to sleep, and laughed. "I wish I could have seen that."

"Thomasina was something." Denton shook his head. "Maybe I'll look her up while I'm in Houston."

"You should do that. I bet she'd be glad to see you."

Denton was still shaking his head, back and forth, like a swimmer who had water in both ears. "I guess you got somebody coming to meet you at the station when you get to wherever it was in Texas you said you was going," he said.

"Uh, yeah. Sure. My mom will come get me." He hadn't exactly thought that far ahead. He hadn't told anyone he was going to do this—not his mom, or his dad, either. Maybe at the next stop, he'd look for a phone and call home, just so his dad wouldn't worry. Then when he got to Tipton, he'd call Grandpa's house and let Mom know he'd arrived.

"Ain't nobody coming to meet me." Denton pressed his forehead against the window and stared out into the darkness. "I done my time and the state turned me loose. They gave me one new suit of clothes and a bus ticket to wherever I wanted to go, and that's it."

"That's tough." Casey didn't know what to say. He wondered if he could pretend to go to sleep again.

Denton raised his head and looked at him again. "You got any money, kid?"

The hair rose up on the back of Casey's neck and his heart pounded. Denton didn't have a gun in his hand or anything, but the way he said those words, you just knew he'd said them before when he *did* have a weapon.

"I got a little," he mumbled. He had a little over thirty dollars in his billfold in his backpack. Enough to buy meals the rest of the trip, he guessed.

"I saw you eating dinner when we stopped back there, so I figured you had money. You ought to give me some money so I can buy some dinner. You ought to help out a fellow traveler."

Casey wondered if Denton was telling the truth.

Would the state turn somebody loose with no money in his pocket? That seemed like a sure way for someone to end up back in jail really quick. Maybe Denton was just trying to scam him.

"When we stop again, I'll get some food and we can share it," he said. He fought back a grin, proud of the way he'd handled the issue. But then, he'd always been good at thinking on his feet. It was another talent he knew would come in handy throughout his life.

Denton grunted, apparently satisfied with this answer. He rested his head against the window and closed his eyes and was soon snoring.

Casey slept, too. The rocking motion of the bus and the darkness, punctuated by the whine of passing cars and the low rumble of the bus's diesel engine, lulled him into a deep slumber. He dreamed he was wandering through the streets of Tipton, searching for his grandfather's house, unable to find it.

When Karen returned from the grocery store, the aide, an older black woman named Millie Dominic, met her at the door. "Mr. Martin is carrying on something fierce, but I can't figure out what he wants," she said.

Karen dropped the bags of groceries on the kitchen table and ran to her father's bedroom. He was sitting up on the side of the bed, one foot thrust into a scuffed leather slipper, the other bare. When he saw her, he let out a loud cry and jabbed his finger toward the chair.

"I asked him if he felt up to going outside for a walk and he *roared* at me," Mrs. Dominic said.

"I think he wants to go back to his office." She looked at her father as she spoke. At her words, he relaxed and nodded.

"What's he gonna do in there?" Mrs. Dominic asked as she helped Karen transfer Martin to the wheelchair.

"He can work on his computer. He types with his right hand, so he can communicate." She lifted his left foot onto the footrest and strapped it in place. "I guess that's less frustrating for him."

Once at his desk, he waved away Karen's offer of a drink, but she brought him a Coke anyway, with a straw to make it easier to sip. He was alarmingly thin, and the doctor said she should try to get as many calories into him as possible.

She thanked Mrs. Dominic and sent her on her way, then began putting away groceries. At home right now she'd be answering phones for their business while trying to decide what to cook for supper. If Casey was around, he'd suggest they have pizza. He would have gladly eaten pizza seven days a week.

How were Tom and the boys managing without her? Was paperwork stacking up on her desk at the office, while laundry multiplied at home? *We need you here.* Tom's words sounded over and over in her head, like an annoying commercial jingle that refused to leave, no matter how hard she tried to banish it. He'd sounded so…accusing. As if she'd deliberately deserted them in favor of a man who had earlier all but abandoned her.

No matter what Tom might think, she'd never desert her family. They were everything to her. But she couldn't turn her back on her dad, either. He was still her father, and he needed her. Maybe the only time in his life he'd needed anyone. She might never have a chance like this again.

She decided to make corn chowder, in the hopes that her father could eat some. Though he'd never been a man who paid much attention to what he ate, content to dine on ham sandwiches for four nights in a row without complaint, she thought the diet of protein drinks must be getting awfully monotonous.

After living so long with three boisterous, talkative men, the silence in the house was getting to her. She started to switch on the television, then at the last minute turned and headed for the study. Her father couldn't form words, but as long as he could type, they could have a conversation. It was past time the two of them talked.

"Hey, Dad," she said as she entered the room.

When he didn't look up, she walked over and stood beside him. "What are you doing?"

He glanced up at her, then leaned back slightly so she could get a better view of the monitor screen. He'd been studying a spreadsheet, listing birds by common and scientific names, locations where he had seen them, columns indicating if he had tape-recorded songs for them. Birds he had never seen were indicated in boldface. There weren't many boldfaced names on the list.

"Mom said you had just seen a Hoffman's Woodcreeper when you had your stroke," Karen said.

He moved the mouse back and forth, in jerky motions, until the cursor came to rest on the entry for the Woodcreeper. It was no longer boldfaced, and he had dutifully recorded the time and date of the sighting.

"That's great, Dad. You've done a phenomenal job."

He shook his head, apparently not happy with her praise. She wasn't surprised. As long as she could remember, he hadn't been satisfied. When he was home, he was always planning the next expedition, making list after list of birds he had not yet seen, counting and recounting the birds he *had* seen, and frowning at whatever number he had reached so far.

In addition to the life list of all the birds he'd ever seen, he also kept a yard list of birds seen at his home, a county list, state list, as well as various regional and country lists. This accumulation of numbers and ordering of names seemed to be almost as important to him as the birds themselves. Maybe more so.

He closed the spreadsheet and opened a new file. Using the index finger of his right hand, he slowly typed in a number: 8000.

Karen nodded. "The number of birds you've been trying for."

He typed again: 7,949.

She studied the number, wondering at its meaning. "The number you've reached on your list?"

He nodded, and punched the keyboard again. Another number appeared on the screen: 1.

She shook her head. "I don't understand. What's the one for?"

He grunted, and typed again: Brazil.

"One more bird you haven't seen in Brazil." Her eyes met his, and the anger and pain she saw there made her stomach hurt. Her father was so upset over a single species of bird that had escaped him in Brazil. Had he ever cared so much about another person? About *her*?

She patted his shoulder. "I'm sorry you didn't get to clean up Brazil while you were there. But the doctor says you should be able to regain a lot of function on your left side, and you can learn to talk again. Going back to Brazil and finding that bird can be your motivation." Never mind staying around to see his grandchildren grow up, or to enjoy his own children in his old age. Some people were inspired by goals like that; for her father, the only thing that mattered were birds.

The next morning, very early, the phone rang, jolting Karen from sleep. She groped blindly for the receiver, her hand closing around it as her other hand reached for the light. "Hello?"

"Have you heard from Casey?" Tom asked, without bothering to say hello.

The urgency in his voice jerked her wide awake. She sat on the side of the bed and clutched the receiver with both hands, heart pounding. "No. Why? What's going on?"

"He went out walking before supper last night and hasn't come home."

Fear, like a freezing wind, stole her breath. She stared at the phone, as if she were staring down the barrel of a gun. "What do you mean, he hasn't come home?"

"Just what I said. At first I thought he was at a friend's house, or was staying late at the mall, but I've called everyone he knows and driven all over town looking for him and no one knows anything."

News stories of missing children flashed through her mind, the headlines stark and chilling: *Abducted. Missing. Gone.*

"Karen, are you still there? Have you heard from Casey?"

Tom's words jolted her to life again. She forced herself to breathe deeply. Now was no time to fall apart. "No, I haven't heard anything." She looked at the clock. 6:00 a.m. Five in Denver. Tom must have been up all night. "Was he upset when he left? Did you have a fight about something?"

"No. We hadn't talked at all since morning, when I'd agreed to let him apply for the lifeguarding job. He seemed happy about that."

"What does Matt say?"

"He says Casey seemed fine. I don't know what to think."

Tom's voice was ragged with exhaustion. She imagined him, unshaven, running his fingers through his hair the way he did when he was upset. Of course he had handled this for hours by himself. "Maybe you'd better call the police."

"I already did. They promised to keep an eye open, though they're treating it like a runaway situation."

"Why would Casey run away?" Granted, he didn't like school, but he'd always been happy at home. Things that would get other kids down didn't seem to touch him. More than once, she had envied her youngest son his easygoing demeanor. "Maybe he has a friend we don't know about, and he's staying with them."

"Maybe. His backpack is gone, and Matt thinks he took some money with him, but his clothes are still here."

"He's probably with a friend." He had to be. Surely he wouldn't be one of those kids you read about in the news—children abducted by strangers. She resolutely shoved the thought away.

"If he was going to stay with a friend, he should have called us."

"He should have. But you know Casey. He doesn't

think about things like that." When he was little, she could always find him in the house by following a trail of his belongings to the room he occupied. She used to berate him for being so inconsiderate, but he'd look at her with genuine confusion. "I wasn't doing it to be inconsiderate," he'd say. "I was just thinking about other things."

That was Casey, head in the clouds all the time, dreaming big dreams no one else could comprehend. Lost in thought, had he stepped off a curb and been hit by a car? "Did you...did you check hospitals?" she asked, her breath catching on the words. "Maybe he's been hurt and can't call."

"I'll do that as soon as I get off the phone with you. I'm sorry to worry you, but I was hoping you'd heard from him. He talks to you about things more than he does me."

And if I was home, maybe this wouldn't have happened. The unvoiced accusation hung between them.

"Please, let me know if you hear anything."

"I will." He sighed. "I'd better go."

After he hung up, she cradled the receiver to her chest, fighting tears. Casey might be sixteen years old, but he would always be her baby; the sweet, contrary boy, the child she worried about the most.

Tom was right—Casey did confide in her more. If she'd been home, he might have talked to her about whatever was bothering him. And if she'd been there, she could have run interference between him and his father. Though Tom denied it, she was still convinced he'd said something to upset their youngest son. Casey was sensitive, and Tom had a way of saying hurtful things without even meaning to.

Every part of her wanted to get on a plane and fly straight to Denver. Surely she, his mother, would be able to find him when others had failed.

But the sensible part of her knew that wasn't true. And if she went back to Denver, who would look after her father? She couldn't count on Del for anything, and her mother was too self-centered and argumentative to last for long. Within half an hour, Mom and Dad would be fighting, and only sheer luck would keep her dad from having another stroke.

They could all use a little luck now. She closed her eyes and sent up a silent prayer for Casey's protection. *Please let him be all right. Please let us find him soon.*

She was still sitting on the side of the bed, eyes closed, when she heard the bell ringing. She'd given it to her father yesterday, so he could summon her without resorting to banging on the furniture. The ringing meant he was awake, and impatient for something. She sighed, stood and reached for her robe. Somehow, she'd get through this day. Whether she did it without snapping someone's head off or raiding the liquor cabinet remained to be seen.

Casey woke with a start when the bus pulled into the station in Texarkana, Texas. The sign identifying the stop glowed dull red in the hazy gray dawn. Casey squinted at it, rubbing his eyes. He yawned and stretched his arms over his head, then realized the seat beside him was empty. Skinny Denton must have slipped past him and gone into the station to use the men's room or something.

He retrieved his backpack from the overhead bin and went in search of breakfast. He'd buy enough to share with Denton, and maybe some snacks for later on down the road.

He hit the men's room first, and washed his face and combed his hair. He stroked a finger over the faint moustache showing over his upper lip, and ran his palm along his jaw, hoping to feel some sign of whiskers there.

He hadn't packed a toothbrush, so he swished his mouth out with water, then headed for the station cafeteria. He looked for Denton, but didn't see him. Maybe he was already back on the bus.

In the cafeteria, he filled his tray with two breakfast sandwiches, two muffins and two cartons of milk. At the cash register, he added two cellophane sleeves of peanuts, for later.

"That'll be $12.67," the woman at the cash register said.

He reached in the outside pocket of the backpack for his wallet, shoving his hand all around inside when he didn't feel it right away. "Must have put my wallet inside the pack last night," he mumbled, and slung the pack off his shoulder to search the main compartment.

A good minute of searching proved fruitless. Feeling sick to his stomach, Casey looked at the woman. "I think somebody stole my wallet."

She frowned at him, and looked pointedly at the food on his tray. "You gotta pay for this," she said.

He looked down at the food, too sick and angry to eat it now, anyway. "I'm sorry. I can't." He shoved the tray away from him and fled the diner, running all the way back to the bus.

As he'd expected, Denton wasn't there. He looked around at the other passengers, half hoping to see Denton in another seat. But there was no sign of the con. "Anybody seen the guy who was sitting here? Real skinny dude, plaid shirt?"

A few people looked at him. Even fewer shook their heads, then went back to reading or napping or whatever they'd been doing.

"Bastard stole my wallet!" Casey said, louder now. Denton had probably taken the wallet and slipped out while Casey slept. "Somebody must have seen him."

No one looked at him now. Casey punched the back of the seat, hard. His hand stung almost as much as his eyes. He blinked back tears of frustration and sagged into his seat as the bus lurched forward. Chin on his chest, he stared out the window. He'd been such an idiot! He should have kept his wallet with him, and kept his mouth shut about having any money. He never should have talked to Denton in the first place.

Maybe Matt was right. Maybe he was a big loser.

A young woman had flown with Martin on the air ambulance that had transported him to Texas from Brazil. She was a nurse, he supposed, and her name was Karen, too. Her name was printed on a badge she wore on her crisp blue uniform, a uniform the color of a jay's wing.

He'd been strapped into a stretcher before they brought him onto the little plane. He'd fought against the restraints, hated being confined. He wanted to sit up, but he couldn't find the words to tell this Karen. When he'd tried to raise himself, he could only flounder weakly.

She'd rushed to calm him, her voice soothing, her eyes full of such tenderness he'd started to weep. She'd patted his hand and brushed the hair back from his face until he fell into a drugged sleep.

His Karen did not look at him that way. Her eyes held suspicion. Caution.

It seemed to him his daughter had been born holding back. She'd been almost two weeks late in arriving into the world. The doctors had been discussing inducing labor when Sara's contractions finally began in earnest.

Later, after she'd been cleaned up and swathed in a diaper and gown and knit hat and booties, a nurse had thrust her into his arms. He'd looked at her, terrified. She seemed so impossibly small and fragile. She'd opened her eyes and stared up at him with a grave expression, as if even then she didn't trust him to look after her.

Sara had taken over after that—feeding and fussing and diapering, shooing him out of the way.

He'd done what his own father had done, what most of the other fathers he knew did back then. He'd stayed out of the way. He'd gone to work and turned his paychecks over to Sara.

He'd come home from business trips and in his absence the two children (Delwood had been born by this time) and his wife had formed a cozy family unit in which he was the outsider.

He remembered once volunteering to dress Karen, then about three, while Sara fussed over Del. Within five minutes, his daughter was in tears and he looked on, dismayed, with no idea what to do.

"Not that dress. She hates that dress." Sara rushed into the room, Del tucked under one arm, and snatched the offending garment from Martin's hand. "And she can't wear those shoes. They're too small. Go on." She shooed him from the room. "I'll take care of this. Wait for us outside."

The outdoors became his retreat. Those were early days, when he still thought of birding as a hobby. He knew he was good at it. Already his list numbered over a thousand birds. But as he spent more and more time searching for difficult-to-find species, and as he began to gain recognition from fellow birders, the idea of being one of the elite big listers became more and more alluring.

Here was his talent. His niche. The one place where he wasn't dismissed as incompetent or unnecessary. He wasn't blind to the knowledge that the records and rewards had come at a price. He was aware of how dearly he'd paid whenever his daughter looked at him and he saw the doubt in her eyes.

But it was easier to go out again and search for a rare species of bird than to overcome those doubts after all these years. Easier and, for him at least, the outcome was more certain.

Casey smoothed back his hair, straightened his shoulders, then pushed open the door of the lunchroom at the Houston bus station. A few customers waited in line at the cash register, but the lunch counter was empty save for the burly man who stood behind it.

"Excuse me, sir?" Casey remembered to speak up and look the man in the eye. Dad always said people trusted you more if you looked them in the eye.

"Yeah?" The man didn't look very happy to see Casey but then, he was probably one of those people who weren't happy in general.

"I was wondering if I could wash dishes or sweep up

or something, in exchange for a meal." Casey thought the approach was right—not too cocky, but not too downtrodden, either.

The man's expression didn't change. "If you want a meal, you'll have to pay for it."

"That's how it usually works, isn't it? Only thing is, my money was stolen." He took a few steps closer, gaze still steady on the man behind the counter. "I had my wallet in my backpack and this ex-con who was sitting next to me on the bus lifted it while I was sleeping."

The man shook his head. "You should have known better than to put your wallet somewheres where he could get his hands on it."

"Yeah, I should have. Guess I learned my lesson about that one." He shrugged. "So here I am, one dumb kid, not quite as dumb as when I started out on this trip."

The man seemed to think that was funny. He chuckled. "Where you headed?"

"To Tipton." He took a chance and slid onto a stool in front of the man. "I'm going down to help my mom look after my grandpa. He had a stroke."

"That's too bad. How old a man is he?"

He calculated in his head. "He's seventy. But he's never been sick before, so this took everybody by surprise."

"Where you from?"

"Denver. It's a long bus ride from here, that's for sure."

"Yeah." The man looked at him for a long moment.

Casey waited, hardly daring to breathe. Finally, the man nodded. "I reckon I could fix you a burger. While I'm cooking it, you can sweep the floor."

Casey hopped up. "Thanks!"

"Yeah, yeah." The man waved him away. "Broom's over there."

Casey found the broom and began sweeping around the front counter and the tables beyond. As he worked, he hummed to himself. He didn't feel like a loser anymore. He felt like someone who'd found a way to look after himself. He wasn't even that mad at Denton. Maybe the state really had cut him loose without a cent. The guy probably did need that money more than Casey did. After all, Casey had talents. A man with talent would always get by.

CHAPTER 4

When one thinks of a bird, one fancies a soft,
swift, aimless, joyous thing, full of nervous energy
and arrowy motions—a song with wings.
—T. W. Higginson, The Life of Birds

Karen didn't know if her father woke up in a rotten mood, or if her own anxiety over Casey made her impatient with him, but for whatever reason, getting Martin up and dressed was a battle. He rejected the first two shirts she chose for him before grudgingly relenting to the third, then refused to allow her to wheel him to the breakfast table, insisting on going to his study instead.

Anger burned like acid in her throat as she watched him switch on the computer, his gaze fixed on the screen as he waited for it to boot up. He apparently hadn't noticed how upset she was, or if he had, he didn't care enough to ask what was wrong. A person didn't need the power of speech to show someone he cared.

"You don't care about anyone but yourself, do you?" she snapped. "Yourself and birds you can add to your list."

He looked up and blinked, confusion in his eyes.

"Don't pretend you don't know what I'm talking about." She moved closer and bent over to look him in the eye. "You would rather sit in front of that computer all day, playing with your charts and numbers, than have a conversation with your own daughter."

He frowned, then tapped something out on the keyboard. She looked at the screen.

Can't talk.

"You can type, though. We can communicate that way. And you could listen, if you wanted to."

Still frowning, he typed again.

What do you want to talk about?

"We could talk about anything. The topic doesn't matter. We could talk about…" She looked around the room, searching for some likely topic, then decided on the one that had been utmost in her mind all morning. "We could talk about your grandsons."

Casey and Matthew.

"I'm glad to see you still remember their names."

How are they?

"Matthew is fine. Helping Tom with the business. He's planning on going to college part-time next semester."

What about Casey?

"Casey…" She looked away, unnerved by the knot of tears clogging her throat. "Casey…" She tried again, but could only shake her head.

What?

She cleared her throat and took a deep breath. "Tom called this morning. Casey's...disappeared. I mean, we don't know where he is right now."

Martin's right eyebrow rose and he leaned toward her, his expression demanding to know more.

"I don't know." She held out her hands, a gesture of helplessness. Exactly how she felt. "Tom says he didn't come home last night. He's not with his friends...."

Her father stabbed at the keyboard again.

He's run away?

"Maybe. I don't know. It's so unlike him." Casey wasn't one of those moody, belligerent teenagers who made life so difficult for some of her friends. He was always easygoing, uncomplaining—happy, even.

He's upset because you're here.

"No, he isn't. He was fine when I talked to him yesterday morning." Why did he automatically assume this was her fault? "He's probably staying with a friend and forgot to mention it to Tom." She refused to believe Casey had deliberately run away—or worse, that someone had harmed him.

Police?

"Tom says he notified them. I'm sure they'll locate him soon." She hugged her arms across her chest. "Are you ready for breakfast?"

Coffee.

"I could use some coffee, too." She went around to the back of his wheelchair and started to roll him toward the kitchen, but he put his right hand out to stop her.

I'll eat here.

She frowned at him, but he matched the expression and shook his head, then turned his attention once more to the computer screen.

She turned toward the kitchen to make coffee. So much for thinking he might want to stay with her, to keep her company in her distress, or to share his own concern over his grandson. Her father dealt with this trouble as he had with every crisis in his life, by retreating to his charts and birdcalls, to the logic and order of tables and numbers.

And Karen had nowhere to retreat, nothing that offered escape from worry and frustration.

Martin had once spent the better part of two days sitting in a blind on the edge of a Scottish lake, waiting for the arrival of a pair of rare King Eider ducks which had reportedly been recently spotted in the area. His patience had been rewarded near dusk on the second day. The sight of the stocky black-and-white male and his dark brown mate gliding over the shrubby willows at the edge of the lake to land on the wet pewter surface had erased the aching from his cramped limbs and made the long wait of little consequence.

He had not been born with that kind of patience, but he had learned it as a necessary skill for success as a serious birder. And he had found the same stoicism practical in everyday life.

He knew his daughter thought him cold and callous. He didn't have the energy to explain to her that he saw no point in becoming overly emotional and fretting. Wringing his hands or storming about wouldn't help her locate her boy.

He was sorry to hear Casey was missing. Though he hadn't seen the boy in a few years, he remembered his youngest grandson as a thoughtful, intelligent boy who'd shown an interest in birds and the ability to sit still for long periods of time, contemplating the world around him. Martin thought he had the potential to be a big lister, if he applied himself.

He moved the mouse to click on the desktop icon to open his e-mail account. The stroke had temporarily incapacitated him, but that didn't mean he couldn't stay abreast of news in the birding world. Besides, focusing on birds was calming. There was order and logic in the neatly aligned spreadsheets of birds he had seen and birds he had yet to see, deep satisfaction in the number of sightings on each continent, in each country, and within each genus. Reading through these familiar lists would be a welcome distraction from worries about one boy who was currently unaccounted for.

But first, the e-mail.

ABA recognizes Cackling Goose.

His interest sharpened when he spotted this header, and he clicked on the message. He'd been waiting for this one after hearing rumors for the past six months. Birds that were previously considered subspecies were sometimes awarded full species status, thus adding to the total of species in existence. His hand shook as he scrolled through the press release a birding acquaintance had pasted into the e-mail. The Canada Goose, *Branta canadensis*, had been split into large and small species, the smaller birds now being designated *B. Hutchinsii*, Cackling Goose.

Quickly, he shrank the e-mail file and opened his spreadsheet for North American birds. Triumph surged through him as he verified that he had seen both versions of geese at various times and locations. This allowed him to add the new bird to his life list.

He leaned toward the keyboard, straining to control his movements, to type in the new name beneath the original species. Working one-handed was laborious; several times he had to erase what he'd written and start over.

By the time he sat back and studied the new entry, sweat beaded his forehead and he was breathing heavily. His gaze dropped to the new total at the bottom of the spread sheet. Seven thousand, nine hundred and fifty.

He might reach eight thousand yet, even if his health forced him to give up traveling. New species were added every year. In the last year he'd added almost a dozen to his count. Long-dead big listers continued to add to their records through this process. Still, accumulating sightings this way was not the same as seeing new birds for himself.

He scrolled through the list, each name bringing to mind a successful hunt. He'd sighted the King Eider on a miserable cold day when the fog had settled around their party of both serious and casual birders like a shroud. The others in the group retired to a pub to banish the chill with pints of beer and glasses of malt whisky. But he'd insisted on staying outside, willing the bird to come to him.

It had arrived like an apparition out of the mist, the ink black body sharp against the gray fog, the orange shield above its bill brilliant against the bright blue crest. Martin held his breath, immobile, transfixed by this glimpse of the divine. Was it so far-fetched to think that a creature with wings was one step lower than the angels?

The King Eider was the fourth new species he'd added to his list that day. Number 3,047. In those days, he'd seen four thousand birds as a lofty goal to attain. Only later, when he'd passed four thousand and was closing in on five thousand, did he begin to think of reaching for more. Of trying to do what almost no one before him had done.

When he'd joined the others in the pub, they had

groaned at the news of the sighting, and cursed his luck even as they bought him drinks. No one questioned that he had actually seen the bird. Though worldwide, the birding community was a small one, where honesty and integrity counted for everything. Martin's reputation was unassailable. Others often said no one worked harder or was more dedicated than Martin Engel.

The respect of his colleagues was almost as important to him as the numbers on his list. When he was a child, he had sometimes felt invisible in the midst of his older and younger siblings. Their names were routinely in the local paper as winners of athletic competitions and academic honors. Trophies and award certificates lined shelves in the family room. Only Martin had no plaque or statue with his name on it. The family photo album was devoid of Martin's accomplishments, for there were none. His parents, busy with their other talented children, had left Martin to himself. Sitting in the bleachers at the innumerable football, baseball and soccer practices of his siblings, he had discovered birds, and what grew to be an avocation, an obsession—a calling.

He glanced at the framed awards that filled one wall of his office. His parents were no longer alive to see these honors. He seldom saw his siblings, and even his children took little notice of his accomplishments most days. It didn't matter as long as his fellow birders applauded him, and as long as he himself could look at this tangible evidence of all he'd achieved and feel satisfaction filling him, warm and penetrating as the African sun.

When he was gone, the records he'd set would live on. His grandsons could find his name in books and on Web sites, and they'd know that he'd been more than an odd little man who traveled a great deal and didn't have much to say. They'd see that he'd made his mark on the world, and maybe they would find a way to make their mark as well.

Fortified by coffee and toast, Karen called her mother to give her the news about Casey. *I'm not in right now.* Sara's voice on the answering machine was soft and high-pitched, like a young girl's. *I hope it's because I'm out having a marvelous time. Leave a message and I'll get back to you as soon as I'm able.* That was Sara, determined in retirement to make up for what she had once referred to as "the dull and dutiful years" as wife and mother.

"Mom, I've got some bad news. It's about Casey. He…he's missing. He may have run away or something. Call me." She hung up the phone and stared at the receiver, agitation building. Not knowing what was happening was eating her up inside. She wanted to be there with Tom, talking to the police, questioning Casey's friends. Instead she was stuck here. Helpless.

She snatched up the receiver and punched in Tom's

cell number. He answered on the second ring. "Hello?" His voice was gruff, anxious.

"It's me. I was wondering if you'd heard anything new."

"Someone reported a boy who looked like Casey hanging around the bus station yesterday afternoon. The police are trying to determine if he got on a bus, and where it was headed."

She sagged against the counter, and hugged one arm tightly across her middle, as if to hold in the nauseating fear that clawed at her. "Where would he go? And why?"

Tom sighed. "That's what the police keep asking me and I don't know what to tell them. All I can think is that he got some wild idea and acted on it. Maybe he's going to Hawaii to be a surfer or to California to be a movie star. The kid always has his head in the clouds."

"He means well. And he's still young." Yes, Casey was irresponsible and immature. But what was wrong with letting him enjoy his dreams while he still could?

"He's sixteen years old. It's time he grew up."

She refrained from rolling her eyes. This was a familiar litany of Tom's. Now was not the time to get into that discussion. "Call me if you hear anything else, okay?"

"I will."

She had scarcely hung up the phone when her mother's bright blue Mustang convertible pulled into the driveway. Sara breezed up the steps and into the house without knocking. "Good morning, darling," she said, depositing an air kiss to the left of Karen's cheek. "How are you this morning?"

She stepped back, and one look at her daughter had her shaking her head. "Is it that bad already? I was hoping—"

"Mom, did you get my message?"

"What message?"

"My phone message. I just called you."

"I haven't been home. I was having breakfast with Midge Parker. She tried to talk me into going to play tennis with her and Peggy Goldthwait, but I told her I had better see how things were getting on with you. Is your father being a tyrant?"

"No. I'm not upset about him. It's Casey. He's missing."

"Missing?" Sara's perfectly plucked eyebrows arched higher.

"He didn't come home last night. The police think he might have run away. Someone saw him—or at least a boy who looked like him—at the bus station."

Sara put her arm around her daughter and steered her toward the sofa. "I'm sure you're terrified, but everything will be all right. Casey is a smart kid. He knows how to look after himself."

"He's only sixteen. He looks like a man, but he's still a boy." Karen leaned against her mom, grateful for the strong arm around her. "And he's so…impulsive."

Sara smiled. "I remember when you ran away once."

Karen's mouth dropped open and she stared at her mother. "I never ran away."

"Oh, yes, you did." Sara nodded. "You were nine years old and you told me you were going to find your *real* family."

The memory returned with a jolt. "I packed my Barbie suitcase," Karen said. She recalled the contents—two Barbie dolls, a flower identification book, her toothbrush, a change of underwear, four dollars and ninety-three cents in change, a Chapstick and a map of Texas she'd swiped from the glove compartment of her mother's car.

"You got as far as the Piggly Wiggly parking lot and Barbara Anne Jones from church saw you and talked you into letting her give you a ride home."

By the time Mrs. Jones found her, Karen had spent half her money on a package of Oreos and a pint of milk. She'd reasoned she'd be more likely to recognize her real family on a full stomach. "You gave me a spanking and made me clean out the hall closet as punishment."

"I told you this was the family you were stuck with, so you'd better get used to the idea."

But she never had. Not really. All her life she'd felt out of step with the rest of them. She wasn't interested in birds, like her father, or a daredevil like her brother.

She couldn't talk to anyone about anything the way her mother did.

As a child, she would look in the mirror every night as she brushed her teeth and imagine that somewhere, there was a family with a father who doted on his little girl, and a mother who knew all the girl's friends and everything that happened at the girl's school. Instead of spending all her spare time playing bridge and volunteering at the Y, the mother took the girl shopping for cute clothes, and the father helped her with her homework every evening. And the little girl had no siblings, so she was the center of her parents' attention.

"It'll be all right," Sara said again, and patted Karen's shoulder. "When he gets hungry, he'll come home. Sixteen-year-old boys can't go very long without eating."

She almost smiled. While her mother's complacency often annoyed her, she took comfort in it now. If Sara wasn't panicking, things couldn't be that bad.

"I need sugar," Karen said, standing. "I've got some cake Tammy Wainwright made. Would you like some?"

"You bet. And a big cup of coffee." Sara rose, also, and started to follow Karen to the kitchen, but the staccato beep of a car horn made them both look around.

"Who is that in your driveway?" Sara asked.

Karen shook her head. The battered green truck didn't look familiar. As the women watched, the passenger door opened and a familiar lanky figure slid to the ground. He waved to the driver, then shouldered a backpack and started toward the steps.

Karen blinked, half-afraid her eyes had deceived her.

Sara had no such fears. She looked at Karen and grinned. "Good Lord, is that Casey?"

CHAPTER 5

*A bird doesn't sing because he is happy; he sings
because he has a song.*
—Anonymous

Casey expected his mother would be surprised to see
him, maybe a little annoyed that he hadn't bothered
to call first. He didn't know what to think when she
burst into tears.

"Thank God you're all right," she sobbed, running
to him and pulling him close.

"Well yeah, of course I'm fine." Hungry and a little
tired, but okay. He tried to pull away from her a little.
Not that he thought he was too big for his mom to hug
him, but she was getting his shirt all wet.

She stared at his face, as if to verify that it really was
him. "What are you doing here?"

"I thought maybe you needed some help looking
after Grandpa." He spoke with more bravado than he
felt. As the miles rolled out beneath the bus wheels, the
wisdom of his impulsive decision to take off for Texas

had grown more questionable. His dad, for one, was sure to get bent out of shape about it. What if Mom got upset with him, too?

"Casey Neil MacBride, what do you mean scaring us all to death like that?" His grandmother stood on the top front step, hands on her hips. She looked exactly the way she had when he was little and she'd scolded him for swiping cookies from the cookie jar or tracking mud on her carpet. "Your folks have been worried sick. Your father has the police out looking for you."

"The police?" *Shit!* "Why did he do that? I mean, I know I should have called—I thought about it, but by that time I was almost here." Besides, by then Denton Carver had stolen all his money, so he didn't have change for a pay phone. And since his folks had refused to get him his own cell, there was nothing he could do, "I figured when I got here, I could explain everything."

Mom sniffed, and dabbed at her eyes with a wadded-up tissue. "You'd better start explaining."

"Yes, I'm interested in hearing this one," Grandma added.

He stuffed his hands in his pockets and hunched his shoulders. He wasn't always so good at explaining why he did stuff—not in ways that made sense to his parents. It was like, when you got to be an adult, you quit doing anything just because it felt right.

"Did you and your dad fight about something?" Mom asked.

He shrugged. Dad was always on his case about something. "He wasn't too happy after he heard from the counselor, but you know how he is."

"Then whatever possessed you to come all this way?"

He could hear the exasperation in her voice. How long did he have before real anger set in? "I guess after I talked to you the other morning, I thought you sounded so sad. And then I thought about how I'd feel if I was down here by myself and all. And it wasn't like I had anything big going on at home, so I thought, why not surprise you by coming down here?"

She still wore a pinched expression, like she was trying to keep from crying again—or yelling at him. "You still have a week left of school. I think that's fairly *big*."

"Aw, I was failing anyway." He kicked at the dirt. "Why stick around to make it official?"

She shook her head, but put her arm around him and led him toward the house. At least she hadn't started crying again. He couldn't handle more tears.

"I'm going to go now," Grandma said. "I'll talk to you later."

"Thanks, Mom."

They went into the house. It was like stepping into some kind of time warp. He hadn't been here in, what, three years? Yet everything looked exactly the same. Amazing.

"Are you hungry?" Mom asked. "Did you have anything to eat on the way?"

"I had a burger and fries for lunch." More like a late breakfast, really. He hadn't had the nerve to ask for any more handouts after that. He rubbed his stomach. "I am kind of hungry."

"I'll fix you something to eat. But first, we'd better call your father."

He made a face. "Do we have to?" Dad would freakin' lose it when he heard what Casey had done. The old man never cut him any slack the way Mom did.

"Of course we have to. He's been up all night, worrying about you." She took him by the shoulders and turned him to face her. "You do understand how wrong it was of you to take off like that, not telling anybody?"

He nodded. "Yeah. I'm sorry."

"We didn't have any idea what had happened to you—whether you'd run away, or been abducted by a stranger, or hurt in an accident."

"I said I was sorry. I didn't do it to freak you out. I went down to the bus station to see how much the fare from Denver to Tipton would be, and when I saw there was a bus leaving right away, I thought, why not?" He hung his head. "I thought it'd be a cool surprise for you."

"Oh, honey." She put her hand to his cheek, the anger gone from her expression. "I am glad to see you. But until you have children of your own, you won't understand what an awful, awful feeling it is to know that your son is missing, and no one seems to know where he is."

He hugged her, tight. He hated thinking he'd hurt her. "I know. I screwed up again. But I'm here now. And I really am going to help you." He pulled back. "How's Grandpa?"

"Don't change the subject." She picked up the receiver, but stopped when a series of thumping, dragging noises from the hallway caught their attention.

Casey tried not to stare at the figure in the wheelchair. Grandpa Engel had always been such an imposing man. Not big, but tall and sort of *looming*. Now he looked as if he'd been shrunken and dried into this smaller, withered version of himself. His thick brown hair was now gray streaked with white, and Casey could see his pink scalp showing through in places. Only his eyes were as black and fierce as ever. Casey stood up straighter and raised his voice a little. "Hi, Grandpa. It's good to see you up and about."

The old man scowled at him, then looked at his mom and pointed at Casey.

"He got on the bus to come see us, but forgot to tell his father, or anyone else, where he was going."

"Humph!" Or at least, that's what it sounded like his grandfather grunted. Mom had said he couldn't really talk, but he didn't seem to have too much trouble getting his point across. He held up a coffee cup and waved it at Casey's mom.

"I'll make a fresh pot as soon as I've spoken with Tom."

Grandpa didn't seem happy with that news, but with his face sort of tugged downward on one side—Casey guessed from the stroke—it was probably hard for him to look really happy about anything. "You want me to wheel your chair somewhere for you to wait for your coffee while Mom's on the phone, Grandpa?" he asked.

His mom put her hand on his shoulder. "You stay right here, young man. You need to talk to your father."

He gave her a pleading look. "Can't I eat first? I defend myself better on a full stomach."

She gave him her you're-not-going-to-pull-one-over-on-me-this-time look and picked up the phone.

Casey slumped against the counter and stared at the floor. He supposed the situation wasn't completely bad. At least when Dad yelled at him this time, he'd be a thousand miles away.

Karen's hands shook as she punched in Tom's phone number, her initial rush of relief at seeing Casey safe and alive giving way to frustration and anger—all underlaid by the tenderness her vulnerable younger son never failed to engender in her. When he'd told her he'd been worried because she sounded sad, and that he'd come to help her, it had been all she could do not to break down into tears again and hold him close. But she couldn't let his no-doubt sincere good intentions negate the very real fright he'd given them all. He'd have to be punished, as soon as she and Tom decided what was appropriate.

Tom answered the phone right away, as if he'd been anticipating its ring. "Honey, it's me," she said. "Casey is here. He's all right."

"He's there? In Texas?"

She glanced at her son, who was slumped against the kitchen counter, arms folded over his chest, head bowed, as if bracing for a blow. "Yes, he showed up a few minutes ago. Someone in town gave him a ride out here from the bus station."

"He took the bus to Texas? What the hell made him do that?"

She sighed. If she knew the answer to questions like that, raising her children would be a lot easier. "You know Casey. It seemed like a good idea at the time, I guess."

"Let me talk to him."

She held out the phone. "Your father wants to talk to you."

He took the receiver, automatically straightening his shoulders before he spoke. "Hey, Dad."

Whatever Tom said made him wince. Karen's own forehead wrinkled in sympathy. She didn't blame Tom for being angry, but he sometimes let his anger get the better of him with the boys. He said hurtful things without thinking about their impact.

"Yeah, I know I should have told somebody," Casey said. "Yeah, I know this means I won't finish the school year. I thought Mom needed somebody to help her. She's here all by herself looking after Grandpa."

Karen's heart contracted again. How could she stay angry with him when he was so concerned about her? His father hadn't been this sympathetic to her position.

"Well, yeah. But Grandpa likes me. It'll be good for him to have me here."

Another long pause while he listened to Tom, the agitation in his expression increasing.

"Just because I don't do everything the way you'd do it doesn't make me stupid." Casey's voice rose, quaking at the end, sounding to a mother's ear as if he was dangerously close to tears.

She put her arm around him. "Give me the phone." She took the receiver from his hand. "You go wash up. And take Grandpa with you."

When Casey and her dad were gone, she put the receiver to her ear. "There's no sense yelling at him now," she said. "He's here. He's said he's sorry. We have to decide what to do next."

"Saying he's sorry doesn't mean anything if he's going to keep pulling stupid stunts like this." Tom's anger was barely contained. "My God, he could have been killed on the way down there and we'd never know it."

"But he wasn't. He's okay. And I think he's really sorry."

"What about school? This guarantees he'll flunk his year."

"He seems to think he was going to do that anyway."

"Not if he buckled down and got an A on his finals."

"Then maybe we can talk to the school, make arrangements for him to take his finals later. Tell them it was a family emergency. That's not really a lie."

Tom ignored the suggestion. "If he thinks I'm going to let him take that lifeguarding job now, he can forget it. I've a mind to ground him until he's thirty."

"I think we should let him stay here. At least until I come home." The idea had just come to her. Tom's reaction made her reluctant to send Casey back to him. Maybe some distance would make the relationship between father and son less volatile. She couldn't imagine how tense things would be between the two of them without her there to act as a buffer. And it would be good to have him here.

"What's he going to do there? At least here I can put him to work. Maybe have the local police talk to him about what can happen to runaways. Scare some sense into him."

"That's not a bad idea, but it can wait until we're both home. Right now I really could use his help. And maybe a different environment will give him a new perspective."

"He needs more than a new perspective. He's sixteen years old. It's time he showed more responsibility."

"I don't think yelling at him is going to make him grow up any faster."

"Coddling him certainly isn't doing the trick."

She grit her teeth. "Just because I choose to deal

with his behavior rationally, instead of shouting at him, doesn't mean I'm coddling him."

"You're right. I am irrational. If you'd been through what I've been through the last twenty-four hours, you'd be irrational, too."

She pictured him, slumped against the wall, raking one hand through his hair. Maybe if she'd been worrying about Casey for the last twenty-four hours instead of the last six, she'd be more upset, too. "It'll be easier on you if you don't have him to deal with this summer," she said. "And I'll feel less guilty if I'm helping with at least one son."

"Yeah. You're right." He was silent a moment, and when he spoke again, his voice was gentler. "I'm glad he's okay."

"Me, too. Do me a favor and first chance you get, pack up some of his clothes and send them down here. It doesn't look like he brought much with him."

"That figures." He sighed.

"You must be exhausted," she said. "Try to make it an early day, so you can get some sleep."

"Not a chance, not with all the work I have to do. Plus I've got a stack of invoices six inches high that need to be dealt with."

No doubt an exaggeration, but she didn't feel like calling him on it. After all, she'd left everything in perfect order three days ago. Things wouldn't be that far behind—yet. "Call a temp agency and hire some clerical help. You can't do everything."

"I guess you're right." He gave a hoarse laugh. "See, I need you here to figure these things out."

This admission made her relax a little. "I'll be home as soon as I can. Dad's doing really well, so I'm hopeful it won't be too long. Now get some rest."

She hung up, then went looking for Casey and her dad. She found them in the study, her father showing Casey his spreadsheets, Casey pretending to be interested.

Or maybe the interest was genuine. "Hey Mom, did you know Grandpa has seen penguins in South America? And something called an Arctic Tern near the north pole?"

"Your grandfather has seen birds on every continent on earth." She showed him the certificate from Guinness. "He's set records which may never be broken."

Casey admired the certificate. "That's cool." He looked at his mother. "What's for lunch? I'm starving."

She laughed. Now they were back in familiar territory. "Let's go in the kitchen and see. Dad, you come, too."

For once, her father didn't argue. He allowed Casey to push him to the kitchen and even accepted a glass of the despised nutritional supplement, after Casey drank some and pronounced it, "Not as bad as I thought it would be. It might even be good if you put some ice cream in it, Mom."

Dad nodded and she laughed. "Now, why didn't I think of that?"

"See, it is a good thing I showed up, huh, Mom?"

"I guess it is." She had to admit, she didn't feel so alone now. She could count on her youngest son to be there to support her when no one else would.

The nurse's aide had just left the next afternoon when Del paid a visit. With him was a young, beautiful girl dressed in low-cut jeans and a tight T-shirt. She had a ring in her navel and another in her left eyebrow, and she made Karen think of the women in magazine ads for designer jeans or exotic perfume—the ones who always looked as if they had either just gone to bed with a man, or were about to.

"Karen, this is Mary Elisabeth."

Mary Elisabeth offered a hand with a ring on each finger. "It's good to meet you. I think it's really great of you to come down here and look after your daddy this way." She had a Texas drawl that would melt butter, and a handshake as firm as any man's.

Was it possible Del had been singing his sister's praises? She looked over at him. He had his head in the refrigerator, probably searching for another beer. She turned to Mary Elisabeth again. The Catholic school-girl name seemed incongruous on the young woman before her. "Thanks."

"If you ever need any help, or just want to take a break or something, give me a call," she said. "I get along great with older folks."

"You do?" Karen looked at Del again. She'd been

sure he was blowing smoke when he'd offered Mary Elisabeth's services. "Why is that, do you think?"

"Oh, I'm a good listener, and I don't get impatient with them like some people. I used to work at a nursing home, so I've seen pretty much everything related to gettin' old that there is to see."

"Where do you work now?" Karen pulled out a chair at the kitchen table and offered it to the younger woman, then sat across from her.

"I work for the city water department. It's not as interesting as the nursing home, but it pays better. But sometimes I think I'd like to go back to school to be a nurse."

"Interesting." How had this seemingly bright, ambitious young woman ever ended up with Del? She was about to ask as much when Casey emerged from the back bedroom, where he'd been taking a nap.

He cut his eyes to Mary Elisabeth and they widened a little, then he looked at Del. "Hey, Uncle Del." He went over to his uncle and gave him a hug.

"Casey, you brat." Del returned the hug, grinning. "What the hell are you doing here?"

"I came down to help Mom. Hey look, I'm as tall as you now." He held his hand over Del's head, showing the tops of their heads were even.

"So what? I can still whip your ass." Del faked a punch. Casey dodged away, laughing.

"Del, honey, aren't you going to introduce me to your good-looking young friend?" Mary Elisabeth turned a dazzling smile on Casey, who instantly blushed to the tips of his ears.

"This is my nephew, Casey. He's sixteen. Way too young for you."

"Some people think you're too old for me." She winked at Casey, who laughed again.

"I thought maybe Mary Elisabeth could meet Dad, see how they get along," Del said.

"He's napping right now," Karen said. "He usually takes a nap about this time every day."

"That's all right. I'll see him some other time," Mary Elisabeth said. "I have to get to work now. But it was nice to meet you." She smiled at each of them in turn, gave Del a peck on the cheek, and sailed out the door.

They were all silent a moment, as if she'd taken some of the air out of the room with her departure.

"Uncle Del, she's *hot*," Casey pronounced.

Del laughed. "Stick with me, boy. I can teach you a thing or two about how to handle women."

"You'll do no such thing." Karen stood and went to the sink, where she busied herself washing up the breakfast dishes. The thought of her playboy brother teaching her son anything sent shivers up her spine. "She seems very nice. Very bright. How did she ever end up with you?"

"Obviously, she has excellent taste."

Karen snorted.

"That was really cool of her to offer to help you with Grandpa," Casey said.

"Yes, it was very nice." But why would a total stranger offer to do something so nice? She turned to Del. "She's not some gold digger out to talk Dad out of his money, is she?"

"You watch too many soap operas." He tossed his now-empty beer can into the garbage. "Mary Elisabeth is just a nice person who likes to help other people. There are still folks like that left in this world, you know?"

"Yeah, I met one of them on my way down here," Casey said. "He ran this restaurant near the bus station and he let me have a burger and fries in exchange for sweeping up for him."

"You didn't have any money with you?" Karen stared at her son.

He shoved his hands in his pockets and looked around the kitchen. "Well, I had some when I started out, but I sort of lost it."

"You lost it?" She sagged against the counter. Tom was right. The boy was completely irresponsible.

"It was stolen, actually." Casey shrugged.

"Stolen?" She stared at him.

"Yeah, well, this ex-con sat next to me, see, and I couldn't move because there weren't any more empty seats and—"

She put her hand over her eyes and waved away the rest of his explanation. "I don't think I want to hear any more."

Casey came over and put his arm around her. "It's okay, Mom. Everything worked out."

"That's right, sis," Del said. "You worry too much."

The rest of the world might be crazy, but she was the one with a problem, because she worried too much. "It's the worriers in this world who get things done," she said. "People who bother to think about problems figure out how to solve them. Not to mention, we're the ones who look after all you 'free' spirits."

"Maybe so, but I know who's having more fun, don't you, Casey?" Del winked at his nephew.

Casey laughed. "Maybe it's a chick thing." He hugged Karen again. "Stick with us and we'll teach you to lighten up. And you never know. Some of your responsibility might rub off on us."

She sighed. "I hear pigs might fly, too."

Casey laughed again, and she managed a smile. Life was absurd sometimes. And this particular corner of Tipton, Texas, had always been the touchstone for most of the absurdities visited upon her. She'd be glad when she could get back to her ordinary life, where she was mostly in control and usually knew in advance how things would turn out. Unlike Casey, Karen wasn't a big fan of surprises.

CHAPTER 6

We're never single-minded, unperplexed, like
migratory birds.
—*Rainer Maria Rilke*, The Duino Elegies

In his dreams each night, Martin strode through the jungles of the Amazon, or across the plains of the midwest, or along the shores of tropical beaches. Everywhere birds came to him, darting and wheeling about, the flutter of their wings and the lilt of their songs the soundtrack for his slumber. Ruby-throated Hummingbirds hovered before him like feathered jewels, and Black-necked Stilts stitched lines of tracks in the sand at his feet. He watched them with a lightness in his heart, as if at any moment he, too, might sprout wings and learn to soar with their grace.

He would wake buoyed by this excitement and anticipation, brought back to earth with a thud by the limitations of his body. The determination that had once enabled him to scale the peaks of the Andes or trek for days across waterless deserts, or endure all manner of hardships in the pursuit of birds for his list now could not will so much as a finger on his left hand to move or words to form on his tongue.

He silently railed at the injustice of being imprisoned by the frailty of his own flesh. His frustration exploded from him with the least provocation. He banged his wheelchair into walls and furniture, not caring what he destroyed. He swept the lunch tray from his desk, dishes shattering, when a slice of ham wasn't chopped fine enough to keep from choking him. He balked at being shaved or having his hair cut until the aide calmly pointed out that only a fool argued with a woman who held a razor to his throat.

And always there was Karen, watching him with such intensity, alternately cajoling and critical. "Dad, you have to eat more." "Dad, you aren't trying." "Dad, come away from that computer. You need your rest."

How did she know what he needed? She hardly knew him. She thought his pursuit of birds all over the world was a waste of time. Oh, she never said as much, but the shuttered expression she assumed whenever the topic of birding came up told him everything he needed to know. She didn't understand that peace could come in focusing on a part of nature so different from himself. She didn't know that beyond the pleasure of accumulating numbers and amassing records, there were the birds themselves, so diverse and diverting. They offered beauty without judgment. They demanded nothing from him.

* * *

Karen had been back in Texas about two weeks and was beginning to settle into a routine when Del showed up on her doorstep with a dog. "Look what I got for you, sis," he said, grinning like a schoolboy who's just handed his teacher an apple with a worm in it.

She eyed the dog warily. The oversize yellow mutt had floppy ears, legs that looked too long for its body and feet the size of Mason jar lids. It grinned up at her, tongue lolling, reminding her of Pluto from the Disney cartoons of her childhood. "What did you bring me?" she asked warily.

"I brought you a dog. Isn't she great?" He patted the dog's side. The animal responded by flopping over onto her back, tail whipping wildly back and forth, all four feet flailing in the air. A flea crawled across the dirty white fur on the dog's stomach.

Karen took a step back. "I don't want a dog," she said. "I especially don't want an overgrown, flea-bitten mutt."

"Aw now, don't be like that." Del shoved past her into the house. The dog followed, toenails clicking on the hardwood floor.

"No!" Karen rushed after them. "Get that beast out of here. I don't want it."

"You need a dog, sis." Del helped himself to a Coke from the refrigerator. The dog followed, eyes fixed on him adoringly. "She'll keep you company."

"I don't need company. And I don't need anything else to look after."

"Living with a dog will teach you to lighten up." As if on cue, the mutt rolled on her back again, and looked at Karen, as if waiting for some sign of approval.

Del bent and rubbed the dog's belly. "How serious can you be around this?" he asked.

She was seriously considering slapping her brother, to try to knock some sense into him. Or at least force him to listen to her. "No, Del. I mean it. Get that beast out of here."

"Hey, where'd you get the dog?" Casey ambled into the kitchen and grinned at the mutt, still on her back in the middle of the floor. He dropped to his knees beside her and began rubbing her belly. "She's a real sweetie, isn't she? Is she yours, Uncle Del?"

"I got her for your mom."

"Really?" Casey's smile grew even wider and he looked back at Karen. "She's great!"

Karen hugged her arms across her chest and frowned down at Casey and the dog, who were now rolling around together on the floor. When the boys were six and nine, they had launched a campaign for the family to adopt a dog. Tom had been willing to go along with the idea, but Karen had put her foot down, pointing out that if she'd wanted something else to look after, she'd have had another child. The boys and Tom had been wise enough not to press the point.

"No. No dog," she repeated.

Casey's smile crumpled. Crouched on the floor beside the animal, he looked closer to the little boy she remembered than the man he was fast becoming. The image tugged at her heart. "But Mom, why not?"

"Dogs are dirty. They're noisy. They shed. They're destructive. And they need a lot of attention and time I don't have."

"I'll give it attention." Casey sat back on his heels. "Besides, how do you know all that stuff if you've never had a dog?"

"I've known other people who had dogs. A dog is just one more thing for me to look after, and I already have too much to do around here." Between nursing her father and taking care of the house she was stressed to the max already. Not to mention, adding a dog would be one more change in a summer that had brought too many changes to her life already.

"I'll look after her. I promise." Casey threw his arms around the dog and hugged her close. "She won't be that much trouble."

Karen had the feeling things were fast slipping out of her control. She shook her head again. "No."

Casey pretended not to hear her. "Hey, we could maybe train her to help Grandpa. You know, one of those assistance dogs."

The dog seemed intent now on licking the skin off Casey's face. Karen had her doubts this mutt could be trained for anything. "No, I don't want it." She turned to Del. "Get it out of here."

He took a long sip of Coke, then set the can on the counter. "Guess I'll just have to shoot it, then," he said.

"Shoot it?" The outrageousness of the statement left her stammering. "Why…why would you do that?"

"If I take her to the animal shelter, they'll just put her down, plus they'll ask for a 'donation' to do it. A big dog like this is hard to find a home for. A bullet's cheaper."

"Mom, no!" Casey still clung to the dog. The animal herself turned to Karen, eyes the color of chocolate M&M's, filled with sadness. Karen couldn't stand it. Why was everyone making her out to be the villain, when it was Del who'd gotten them into this mess?

She turned to her brother. "Do you even have a conscience? How could you try to foist this dog—that I don't want—off on me, and then threaten to kill her if I don't take her?"

His expression was guileless. "I thought you and Casey, and Dad, too, for that matter, would *enjoy* having a dog around. I saw it as a nice thing to do for you. You're the one trying to make it something bad."

He had had this talent all his life, the knack for twisting words to throw the blame back on someone else. The talent had enabled him to talk his way out of failing grades, traffic tickets, job layoffs and relationship troubles more times than Karen could count. She hated it, but at the same time, she couldn't help but marvel.

Casey rose and stood at her side. "I think Uncle Del had a good idea, bringing us this dog," he said. "This has been kind of a lousy summer for us so far, what with Grandpa being sick and all. A dog like this could give us something to laugh at."

God knows she could use a few laughs. Only she didn't see how a big dirty mutt was going to provide them. She looked down at the dog, who was on her back again, both paws over her nose as if she was hiding her face. It was a ridiculous pose, and Karen felt herself weakening. She still didn't want the animal. She hated being manipulated this way. But she wasn't hardhearted enough to sentence the pup to death, or to risk alienating her son further, at a time when she needed at least one member of her family on her side. She blew out a breath. "All right. She can stay for a little while. But if she causes any trouble, out she goes."

"That's super, Mom." Casey's hug squeezed all the air from her lungs. "I promise I'll help look after her. Come on, girl." He motioned to the dog. "Let's go outside and look around. And we have to think of a good name for you."

The dog trotted after him, tail waving. When Del and Karen were alone again, he turned to her. "I need to talk to Dad. Is he awake?"

"He's on the front porch." Martin liked to sit out

there in the afternoons, alternately napping and scanning the area for birds. "Why do you want to see him?" As far as she could remember, Del hadn't spent a single minute alone with his father since Martin's stroke.

Del arched one eyebrow. "I have to have a reason?"

"No." Though she had no doubt he was up to something. She led him to the porch, half hoping Martin would be asleep. But he looked up as they approached.

"Hey, Dad. How you doing?" Del loomed over his father, his broad shoulders and air of radiant health in sharp contrast to his shriveled, pale sire. Still, Del was the one who looked awkward, head bent, hands clasped in front of him, posture slightly slumped, like a boy awaiting reprimand.

He glanced at Karen. "I need to talk to Dad *alone*," he said.

Translation: *I'm going to ask for something, or propose some scheme that you won't approve of.* She debated staying where she was, ready to defend her father against Del's manipulations.

Martin made a shooing motion with his hand, and grunted, waving her away. Hurt, but determined not to show it, she turned on her heel and fled to the kitchen. Why did she even bother resisting? Del always got his way.

The thought made her feel childish, and she struggled to regain an adult perspective. Del had a right to talk to his father in private. The stroke had left her father physically weak, but mentally he was as strong as ever. It was none of her business what Del did with his life. If she let him manipulate her, it was her own fault for giving in.

The thought rankled. Who wouldn't be annoyed at being manipulated? Why should she take the blame for Del's bad behavior? Maybe that was part of the problem between them—she was too willing to let him get away with being "just Del," too ready to think her own attitude was the one that needed adjusting.

She sagged against the counter, heart pounding. What would happen if she stopped letting the men in her life get away with unacceptable behavior? The idea was tantalizing, and more than a little frightening. Did she really have what it took to be more demanding and less accepting?

"So, you're looking pretty good," Del said when he and Martin were alone.

Martin frowned at the lie, and watched his son, enjoying his discomfort. Del stood awkwardly in front of the wheelchair, as if he was contemplating hugging his father or perhaps shaking his hand.

Martin had no delusions that Del had stopped by out of some concern for Martin's health. The boy never made any pretense of closeness unless he wanted something—to park his trailer on part of the land Martin owned, his father's signature on loan papers for his business, to borrow a car or a tool or money.

Theirs was a relationship of give and take. Martin gave; Del took. They both understood this and were comfortable in their roles.

Del dragged a heavy Adirondack chair over in front of his father and sat, hands on his knees, back straight. "Karen says you still can't talk much."

He couldn't talk at all, which might be an advantage in this instance. He shook his head no.

"Well, I guess you don't need to wear yourself out talking. You can just nod your head and we'll communicate fine." Del's shoulders relaxed a little, as if he liked this idea. "I wanted to ask you a favor," he said.

Martin nodded. Did he know the boy, or what?

"You know Sheila and I split up?"

He nodded again. Del's third wife had surprised him by staying around as long as she had. On Martin's visits home between birding expeditions, he couldn't fail to hear the fireworks from next door; the shouting, tears and slamming doors. Sheila could swear like a sailor, and had once fired a shotgun over Del's head as he and his girlfriend of the moment raced from the trailer one evening when Sheila had arrived home unexpectedly. Martin himself had paid to bail her out of jail that time, and advised her that a load of rock salt and a lower aim might do more good next time.

She had been the best of the Mrs. Del Engels, regularly bringing over casseroles and leftovers, keeping the bird feeders filled when he was out of town, collecting the mail and even mowing the grass Del let grow long. When she hadn't shown up to help since his stroke, Martin had figured Sheila had finally had enough of Del's flirtations and affairs and packed it in. He couldn't blame her, though he would have liked the chance to tell her goodbye.

"Anyway, she's hired some big-shot lawyer and is trying to get pretty much everything I own."

Half of little or nothing hardly seems worth fighting for, Martin thought, doing a mental inventory; the trailer house wasn't worth much, the oil change business was mortgaged to the hilt and, as far as he knew, Del had never had any savings to speak of.

"I told her I couldn't afford to pay what she wanted. She had the nerve to suggest I sell the truck and the motorcycle to get the money."

Martin chuckled. Heaven forbid Del part with his expensive toys.

"You okay?" Del half rose out of his chair, and looked around, possibly for help. "You're not choking or anything, are you? Do I need to get Karen?"

He shook his head and waved the boy back into his seat, then motioned for him to continue.

Del sat, still eyeing him warily. "Anyway, I hired a lawyer who says he can work this so I don't end up in the poorhouse, except he wants five thousand dollars up-front. I just don't have that kind of money."

Unless you sell the truck or the motorcycle.

"So anyway, I was wondering if you could lend me the money. I can pay you back a little at a time, if the business has a good quarter."

The business never had a good quarter, and Del had never paid back more than a hundred dollars of the thousands he'd borrowed over the years. Martin nodded.

"So you'll lend me the money? Great." Del stood, beaming. He glanced toward the door to the house again. "Uh, can you sign a check?"

Martin nodded again. He could sign a check. And then he wouldn't see much of his son until the next time Del was in trouble. It wasn't a very satisfactory pattern for a relationship, but at least it was predictable.

Del left, presumably to get the checkbook, and returned a few minutes later with Karen trailing after him. "Dad, what are you doing, agreeing to give him that kind of money?" she said.

Del sat again, opened the checkbook on his knee and filled in the blanks. "This is none of your business, sis."

Karen turned to Martin. "It's true? You're just going to hand over five thousand dollars?"

Martin nodded. It was his money. If he wanted to piss it away on his shiftless son, that was his business. He took the pen Del offered and bent to inscribe his signature on the check.

Karen folded her arms across her chest and frowned

at them. "I can't believe you're taking advantage of a helpless old man," she said, as if Martin weren't sitting right there.

Martin glared at her, but she didn't notice. She was too busy facing down her brother.

Del let the anger roll off him like steam off wet pavement. He tore the check out of the book, folded it in half and tucked it into his shirt pocket. "Dad's in his right mind, so he isn't helpless. And if he wants to do me a favor, why shouldn't he? I'm his only son."

"You should be ashamed of yourself."

"Shame's a wasted emotion. It doesn't fix anything, change anything or stop anything. I don't see any point in bothering with it." He turned back to Martin. "Thanks, Dad. You take it easy now." He crossed the porch and exited down the steps, whistling as he went.

Karen turned to her father, hurt in her eyes. "How could you? Why do you let him take advantage of you like that? He never does anything for you. He just uses you."

Martin gave because it was easy for him to do so. The money or material goods Del needed didn't mean much to him. He could give them without a second thought. Sign the check, make the loan, hand over the goods and his obligation was met and his relationship with Del returned to normal.

With Karen, things were always more involved. She had always been the difficult child. The needy one. She wanted complicated things—words and emotions. And whatever he surrendered wasn't enough. Time hadn't changed that.

And who was she to accuse her brother of using him? She'd scarcely visited all these years and now that he was helpless, she'd dropped everything and swooped in to run his life. He'd been around long enough to know such sacrifices didn't come without a price. She wanted payment from him in a currency he didn't have in him to pay.

He turned away from her, steering his chair toward the door to his house. All this arguing had tired him. He needed to spend time at his computer. Later, he'd sleep, and be comforted by dreams in which he knew no limitations.

The following Thursday, Karen gave in to Tammy's pleas to have lunch. At 11:30, she found herself seated at Tammy's kitchen table, a glass of iced tea in her hand, a pleasant lethargy enveloping her as she watched her friend bustle about the room. Karen had almost forgotten what it was like to have someone else wait on her, and to not spend every waking moment listening for some signal of distress from her father's room. Or lately, sounds that the dog, whom Casey had named Sadie, was getting into trouble or needed to go out. So far, the dog hadn't made any messes on the carpet—if you didn't count the hair she shed everywhere or the occasional fleas that showed up despite the bath and flea dip Karen had given her. But knowing that she *might* make a mess only added to Karen's stress.

And she could admit, if only to herself, that she'd lost far too much sleep stewing over the five-thousand-dollar *loan* Martin had given Del. While he'd been in talking with their father, she'd told herself she was going to call Del on his impossible behavior, that she wasn't going to let him charm her or browbeat her into meeting his demands.

But in the end, he'd worn her down, defeating her with the argument that while Martin's body might be damaged, his mind was working just fine. If he wanted to give his son money, it wasn't any of her business.

Maybe he was right, but she'd lost more than a few hours wondering what she could have done differently.

"I'm so glad we could get together like this," Tammy said as she chopped celery for chicken salad.

"Thank you for talking me into it." Karen sipped tea, the flavor of fresh mint sweet on her tongue. "It feels so good to get out of the house for a while."

"Now that Casey is here to help you with his grandpa, you should get away more often."

"I never realized what a big help he could be." Karen smiled as she thought of the one really bright spot in the past few weeks. She hadn't spent this much time with Casey since he was a preschooler. Now she had a chance to see a side of him she'd only guessed at before.

"A lot of the time he's more patient with Dad than I am," she said. "And he's better at the messy jobs, like managing bedpans and stuff. And Dad cooperates better for him." Sometimes she wondered if her father wasn't being obstinate on purpose, as if he blamed her for his infirmity, or the indignity of his condition.

"Mo-om, have you seen my new swimsuit?" Tammy's oldest daughter, Sheree, hurried into the room. At seventeen, she was all long legs and straight blond hair.

"In the top drawer, left hand side of your dresser." Tammy added mayonnaise to the chopped chicken and celery and stirred vigorously. "Maybe Casey will be a nurse," she said when the women were alone again.

"Maybe." Karen looked into her half-empty tea glass, as if the answer lay somewhere in the jumble of ice cubes. "He doesn't know what he wants to do."

"Give him time. He's young." She reached into the cabinet overhead and took down two plates.

"Honey, did you pick up those shirts from the cleaners?" Brady stuck his head around the kitchen door. "Oh, hi, Karen. How's your dad?"

"He's a little better. Slow going."

"That's good. And tell Del I said hello." He turned to Tammy again. "My shirts?"

"On the hook on the back of your closet door." She spooned chicken onto slices of bread.

"The videos need returning," Brady said. "I don't have time to do it."

"I'll take care of it this afternoon." She sliced the sandwiches in two and arranged them on the plates. "How is that brother of yours these days?" she asked Karen.

"Aggravating as ever. You'll never guess what he did the other day."

"What?"

"He brought over a dog. This half-grown yellow mutt. Said he got it as a present just for me. As if I needed something else to look after."

Tammy smiled. "What did you do?"

"What could I do? Casey fell in love with the dog the minute he laid eyes on it and Del threatened to shoot it if I didn't take it in." She shook her head. "So now we have a dog. Casey named her Sadie."

"Mo-om! I need ten bucks for the pool." B.J., fifteen, swept into the kitchen, pausing at the refrigerator to help himself to a can of soda.

"In my purse," Tammy said. She set the plate of sandwiches on the table. "Don't forget to wear sunblock. It's in the medicine cabinet."

"I'm tan enough I don't need it." He began eating the rest of the chicken salad directly out of the bowl. "Is there any more of this?"

"No. Don't eat too much if you plan to go swimming."

"I won't." He set the empty bowl in the sink and dropped in his fork. "See you later."

Tammy watched him go, a faint smile on her face.

"When he turned fourteen, it was as if someone threw a switch. He's always hungry. And every time I turn around, his pants are too short." She turned to Karen. "Please tell me it gets better."

"Not for a while, I'm afraid." Karen shook her head. "I'd be happy now if the most I had to worry about was keeping Casey fed. If only he weren't so…so aimless."

"He's a smart kid. He'll figure it out."

"That's what I try to tell Tom, but he thinks Casey should be like him. He had his whole life mapped out by the time he was sixteen."

Sheree hurried past them. "Bye, Mom."

"You be home by six," Tammy called after her. "Call if you need a ride."

"I will."

B.J. and Brady left shortly after that, each receiving instructions and parting hugs from Tammy. Karen took it all in with mixed amusement and awe. Tammy was a general, in clear charge of her territory and her troops. As far back as Karen could remember, this was what her friend had always wanted.

"Did you ever want to do anything else with your life?" Karen asked.

Tammy froze with her sandwich halfway to her mouth. "What do you mean?"

"I mean, did you ever want to be more than a wife and mother? Not that that's bad. You're obviously really good at it. But did you ever wonder if you made the right choices?"

Tammy blinked. "What else would I do?"

"I don't know. I—" They were interrupted by the oven timer dinging.

"I'd better get that." Tammy jumped up from the table. "I promised the Boy Scouts I'd make four loaves of banana bread for the bake sale Saturday," she explained as she opened the oven and peered in at the loaf pans. The banana and walnut odor made Karen's mouth water.

"You could open your own bakery or catering company," Karen said.

Tammy laughed. "And run it in all my spare time?" She shut off the oven and slid the loaves out, one at a time.

"I guess you're right. Who has spare time these days?"

"If I'm not taxiing the kids here and there, I'm cooking or cleaning this place," Tammy said. "Weekends are full of more sports activities and racing."

"I can't believe Brady's still doing that." When they were teenagers, Brady had fixed up an old car and raced it in competitions all over the area. Tammy and Karen had spent many a Friday night or Saturday huddled on sun-scorched bleachers, watching cars race at insane speeds around an oval track.

"Gosh yes. He's in a seniors league now. Lots of guys our age. He's spent three years fixing up his car. You'll have to come see it sometime." She grinned. "Remember the fun we used to have at the track?"

"I remember getting my nose blistered on sunny Saturdays, and flirting with the mechanics in the pit." Karen laughed at the memory. She'd been an awkward teenager desperate to appear sophisticated and older. This translated into a pair of soot-black sunglasses and four-inch platforms that endangered her ankles every time she picked her way across the gravel parking lot to the track. She'd no doubt looked ridiculous, but at the time she was convinced she gave the impression that she was a woman of the world.

"Brady's racing next weekend. You should come with us."

"It would be fun to see the races again. But Casey would probably want to come with me."

"Tell him it's a nostalgia thing—that you're going to relive your childhood. He'll be too mortified to even think of joining you."

"I'll do it." She laughed. "My mother always said the best revenge of parenthood was being able to embarrass your children."

"She's right. Sometimes it's the only revenge." Tammy picked up her sandwich and shook her head. "They have so many ways of getting to us, without even realizing it."

Karen nodded. There was no one who could hurt you like your child, and no one who could bring you as much joy. It was the paradox of parenting, something you never thought about when you were the child.

If pain and joy were barometers of love, then her love for her sons knew no bounds. And her frustration with her father was almost as limitless. Having Casey here brought home the contrast. Sometimes she felt balanced between the two, trying frantically to make life run smoothly for them both.

Unfortunately, neither man appreciated her concern. Why should they, when she never gave them a chance to live without it?

And then there was Tom—the other man who was important to her. She was stuck with trying to placate him long distance, an impossible task. "You've known Brady a long time, haven't you?" she asked.

Tammy smiled. "Since third grade. The first day we met, he threw a spitball at me. I knocked him down on the playground later and sat on him." She laughed. "It was true love."

"So, does he ever say things that surprise you? Things you had no idea he was thinking?"

Tammy tilted her head, considering the question as she chewed. "Not really." She shrugged. "I don't think Brady's a very complicated person. He likes his job. He likes racing and fishing. He loves me and the kids. If something's bugging him, he broods about it a few days and then moves on. We're a lot alike that way. Why? Has Tom surprised you?"

Karen nodded. "I thought he'd understand why I had to come look after my dad. Instead, he's practically pouting because he has to look after Matt and the business by himself for a summer."

"He misses you," Tammy said. "That's sweet."

"He doesn't sound very sweet on the phone. It's like he wants me to *abandon* my father and come home."

"He's probably just feeling a little panicky about looking after everything without you to help. He'll get over it. I'd do the same thing in your shoes. Your dad needs you right now."

Except Tammy would never be in Karen's shoes. Her father lived two blocks away. She saw her parents every Sunday afternoon and countless times during the week.

"I'm trying to talk him into coming down for a visit," Karen said. "Maybe if he sees how helpless Dad is, he'll be more understanding."

"I'm sure he will be. And I know you've missed him."

She *had* missed Tom—especially at night, when she lay alone in her childhood room. But she didn't know what to expect from him these days, or what he wanted from her. They'd been married all these years and there were days when she felt she hardly knew him. They'd been so *busy*—raising the boys, running a business, managing a home—maybe they'd missed out on something important to their relationship, some exercise or habit or activity that would serve as insurance for the years ahead when it was just the two of them again. She wanted to think they could be close in the years to come. Closer than she felt to him right now. What would it take to get to that kind of closeness? Or was that another fantasy, like her dreams of bonding with her dad?

In some ways, her father, for all his sullen silences and uncooperative moments, was easier to deal with than Tom. Having been away from home so many years, she no longer had a fixed role in his life, so there were fewer expectations to live up to.

She sipped iced tea and ate the last of her sandwich. She'd expected to learn a lot about her father while she was here; she hadn't counted on learning so much about herself. For instance, she drew an inordinate amount of satisfaction from the knowledge that whenever she and her father disagreed about something, she was sure to have the final say in the matter. She told herself this was a petty, mean attitude, but there it was. She wasn't always a sweet, nice person. Maturity had taught her to take comfort from that. There was peace in accepting one's faults.

Accepting others' faults was more difficult, as she was learning with her father, and Del, and Tom and even Casey. She hadn't had any luck changing their behavior, but silently accepting it felt wrong, too. What would it take to find her voice and tell them exactly what she thought?

More importantly, how much would the truth cost? Was it a price she was willing to pay?

* * *

Pay attention.

"I am, Grandpa." Casey refrained from rolling his eyes. After all, the old guy couldn't help it if he had to type everything instead of talking.

But his grandfather wasn't the most exciting person to be around even when he wasn't sick. Not to mention that having a *conversation* with him was like being back in school. But it wouldn't kill Casey to humor him. He leaned over the old man's shoulder and studied the spreadsheet on the screen. "You were saying something about the way birds are classified. Families and stuff. I remember that from biology class."

His grandfather stabbed at the keyboard once more, his one-fingered typing surprisingly fast.

Class = aves

Phylum = choradata

Subphylum = vertebrata

Orders = passeriformes (passerines) and non-passerines

He looked at Casey to make sure he understood.

"So every bird in the world is either a passerine or a non-passerine?" Casey asked.

The old man nodded.

23 Orders, 142 Families, 2057 Genera, 9,702 Species

Casey nodded. "I got that. And you've seen close to eight thousand of them."

First you learn the orders, then the families, and so on.

Casey frowned. "But why? I could just learn the names of the birds themselves. Why wouldn't that be enough?"

The old man glared at him, his eyebrows coming together, jutting over his beak of a nose. He looked like a caricature of an angry bald eagle. His hand shook as he typed.

There is a correct way to do this. You must learn the orders first.

"If you're going to get all cranky, I'll leave and go watch TV or something." Casey took a step back. He got enough grief about stuff like this from his mom and dad. He didn't have to take it from somebody he was trying to help, even if it was his grandfather.

Sadie sat up when Casey moved, and looked at him expectantly. The dog was the best thing about his summer so far. She followed him everywhere and had plopped down next to Grandpa's desk as if she'd been living here all her life.

The old man continued to scowl at him, then his shoulders sagged a little. He nodded and beckoned Casey to him once more.

All right. We'll learn names first. But the orders are interesting. When you know the names, you'll want to know the orders, too.

"Fair enough." Casey sat on the corner of the desk and watched as his grandfather highlighted the cells of the spreadsheet. *Ailuroedus buccoides*, White-eared

Catbird. *Ailuroedus melanotis*, Spotted Catbird. *Ailuroedus crassirostris*, Green Catbird.

The old man stared at the funny Latin names like it was some hot porn site or something. He was so enthralled, he'd probably forgotten Casey was even there. Which was okay with Casey. He leaned down and scratched Sadie behind the ears and studied the man at the computer, thinking how odd it was that this was his mom's dad. They didn't look much alike; Mom took after Grandma in the looks department, which he guessed was good. Grandma still looked all right for an older lady. Even before he had the stroke, Grandpa hadn't been all that handsome. He kept himself neat and clean, but he didn't care about stuff like clothes or hairstyles.

But Mom did *act* like her father sometimes. When she was at the landscaping office, working on something on the computer, she had the same kind of intensity Grandpa had now. And she showed her emotions on her face the way Grandpa did. One look in her eyes and you knew she was happy or angry or upset. She never had to say a word.

Uncle Del looked a little more like his dad, at least around the chin and nose. But Casey couldn't imagine someone more different from Grandpa than his mother's brother. Del was real outgoing and friendly. Mom said he was a con artist, so maybe the friendliness wasn't always real, but he sure wasn't the type to spend days alone in the jungle looking for some rare bird the way Grandpa did. And if Uncle Del was mad or glad about something, he'd tell you right to your face.

When Casey looked at his mom and her brother that way, he had to wonder how they ever ended up with the same parents. Then again, he and Matt were plenty different. Matt was the smart, responsible one—just like Dad. Casey thought of himself as the more creative type. An artist, except that he didn't paint or play an instrument or anything like that. Dad couldn't understand him at all, so they clashed all the time.

Mom was easier to get along with, but even she wished he were different sometimes. More ordinary, he guessed. Easier.

Easier for her, that is. He couldn't imagine anything harder than trying to fit into a mold that wasn't right for you.

Grandpa tugged at his sleeve and cocked his head. Casey listened and heard a melodic, gurgling song. Three slow notes, *gluk, gluk, glee!* "I don't recognize it," he said.

Grandpa motioned toward the window, and gave Casey a gentle shove toward it. He shuffled to the glass and looked out. The call came again. *Gluk, gluk, glee!* This time, he saw the chunky, soot-colored bird with the shiny brown hood. "Brown-headed Cowbird," he announced.

Grandpa nodded, his mouth curved into a crooked

grin. He turned to the computer and clicked on a new file. Casey's List was the heading at the top of the page.

"I guess I should add it now, huh?" Casey leaned around the old man and typed in the name of the bird and the time, date and location where he'd seen it. Grandpa added the Latin *Molothrus ater*.

Casey nodded, and admired the new entry. So far the list Grandpa had made for him had only about a dozen birds on it. He'd done it mainly to humor the old man. But he had to admit, it was kind of fun, seeing a bird and noting all the information about it. He didn't know anybody else his age who could identify half a dozen birds, much less more than ten.

Grandpa smiled, and patted his hand. Casey returned the look. At least some people in his life were easy to please.

CHAPTER 7

*I value my garden more for being full of blackbirds
than of cherries, and very frankly, give them fruit
for their songs.*
—Joseph Addison, *the* Spectator

One of Karen's earliest memories was of standing
beside her brother's crib, making faces and laughing
with delight when he smiled at her. Even as a baby, he
had charmed everyone who met him. He had grown
into a sunny child and a willing accomplice in her elaborate games of make-believe.

When had that changed? Had adolescence formed
this gulf between them, or had the divide come earlier,
when she realized that Del's easygoing nature made
him more popular than she would ever be? When he
charmed teachers into overlooking neglected homework assignments while she served detention for
turning in a paper a day late, had that made her see him
in a different light? When he borrowed money and
failed to repay it, dismissing her attempts to collect

with a lopsided smile and a lazy shrug, had that been the final straw?

She caught glimpses of the sweet boy she'd loved even now. On Saturday, he and Mary Elisabeth came to the house with a stringer of catfish and a paper sack of tomatoes, still warm from the vine. "Dinner's on us," he announced, holding up the fish.

"All right!" Casey shut off the television and joined them in the kitchen, Sadie close on his heels. To Karen's surprise, Casey had kept his promise to look after the beast, and Sadie slept each night on the floor beside his bed.

"Del said his daddy loves catfish," Mary Elisabeth said. "And the tomatoes are from my neighbor's garden." She began opening cabinet doors. "I'll cook, if you'll show me where everything is."

"Oh, you don't have to do that." Karen hurried to intercept the young woman as she hefted a cast iron frying pan from the drawer beneath the stove.

"Let her cook, sis." Del steered her toward a chair at the kitchen table and set a long-necked bottle of beer in front of her. "Take a load off."

"You got anything in there for me?" Casey bent and poked around in the blue-and-white plastic cooler Del had deposited by his chair.

"Nothing for you, sport."

Karen studied the bottle in front of her. Sweat beaded on the brown glass and chips of ice clung to the label. She'd been up half the night with her father, who'd developed a worrisome cough, and weariness hung on her like a lead shirt. She couldn't remember when she'd seen anything more enticing and refreshing than that beer.

She raised the bottle to her lips and took a long drink, a sigh escaping her as the icy, slightly bitter liquid rushed down her throat. Del laughed and sat in the chair across from her. "I'd say it's been too long since you let your hair down."

She started to point out that people with responsibilities and some sense of duty didn't have time to *let their hair down*, but the words stuck in her throat. Maybe he had a point. Life couldn't be one big party, as he seemed to try to make it, but neither did it have to be a constant grind, as hers too often was.

Casey slid into the chair between them. "Where'd you catch the fish?"

"Mayfield Lake."

Karen arched one eyebrow as he named a body of water owned by one of the wealthiest families in town. "Isn't that on private property?"

He grinned. "Not if you know the back way in."

His expression was such an exaggeration of fake innocence, she couldn't help but laugh. "And of course, you know the way."

He glanced toward Mary Elisabeth, who was stirring cornmeal and spices in a bowl, humming to herself.

Then he leaned toward Karen, his voice lowered. "I went around with the youngest Mayfield girl for a while. She knew all the places on their land where nobody would bother us."

She took another quick swallow of beer to distract herself from thinking about just what her brother and Miss Mayfield had been up to that they didn't want to be bothered. "You haven't asked about Daddy," she said.

The lines around his eyes tightened and he bent to retrieve another beer from the cooler. "I was going to. How is he?"

"He had a rough night. A bad cough kept him awake."

"He's better this morning," Casey offered. "I think something just went down the wrong way. He still doesn't swallow good sometimes."

Karen glanced toward the string of fish, wet and silver in the sink. "I don't know if fish is such a good idea."

"We'll mush it up for him. It'll be okay." Del popped the top off the bottle. "Where is he now?"

"He's asleep. I'll send Casey to wake him up in a little bit."

"Don't bother him. He probably needs his sleep."

Something in the overly casual way he said the words made her look at him more closely. "You act like you don't want to talk to him."

"It's not like we can have a conversation." He stared

across the kitchen, the muscles along his jaw tense. "Even before he had the stroke we didn't have a lot to say to each other."

"No, he was never much of a conversationalist." She wondered, sometimes, if all those years of sitting silent, watching birds, had taken away the habit of talking.

"I know what you're thinking." Del pointed the lip of the bottle toward her. "You think since I live next door to him, I ought to be over here all the time, checking up on him and playing the dutiful son and all. Well, he didn't want none of that and neither did I. Except for our genes, the two of us don't have anything in common." He set the empty bottle down with a thump.

The bitterness in his voice surprised her. She'd been so focused on her own problems with her father, she hadn't thought much about Del's relationship with him.

Her eyes met Casey's, and he quickly looked away. Had Del's words reminded him of his own uneven relationship with Tom? Her husband rarely hid his frustration that Casey didn't share his interest in the landscaping business or in working on projects around the house. Casey never said anything, but he must have felt his father's disappointment keenly.

It didn't help matters, though, when neither of them would consider the other's point of view—not unlike

Del and Martin. "It's not true that you have nothing in common," she said. "You're both stubborn."

"Oh yeah?" He cocked one eyebrow. "I'd say it runs in the family."

"Del, you need to skin these catfish so I can cook them." Mary Elisabeth confronted him, hands on her hips. She'd tied a dish towel around her waist as a makeshift apron. The towel hung down longer than her shorts, so the effect was of a striped cotton miniskirt.

"Aw, sugar, I'll do it in a minute, don't worry." He reached out and pulled her close, one hand cupping her bottom like he was testing the firmness of a melon.

"I'll do it." Casey jumped up and pushed back his chair.

"You skinned catfish before, boy?" Del asked. "It's not like cleaning one of those Colorado trout, you know."

"I know." He rummaged in the drawer under the phone and came up with a thick-handled knife. He retrieved an enamel dishpan from under the sink, then picked up the stringer of fish. Sadie stood at attention, ears cocked, nose twitching. "You want fillets or whole?" Casey asked.

"Fillets," Mary Elisabeth said. "They're big fish."

When he and Sadie were gone, back door slamming behind him, Del turned to Karen again. "He doing okay?"

"Casey? Why wouldn't he be okay?"

He shrugged. "Seems kind of funny, him showing up here all of a sudden. I mean, what kind of summer is he gonna have, playing nursemaid to a sick old man?"

"He said he wanted to stay with me." She bristled. Did Del think she'd set out to ruin her son's summer?

"Yeah, well, maybe he's a nicer guy than I am." He opened another bottle. "Wouldn't be hard to do, according to you."

"At least he's trying to help."

"And I'm not." He lifted the beer in a mock toast. "Just doing my best to live up to your low opinion of me."

Where had he mastered the art of throwing all blame squarely back on her? He infuriated her, but there was enough truth in his words to choke off her angry reply.

And she didn't want to argue with him right now. She wanted to sit here and let the alcohol buzz smooth out all the rough edges of her emotions. They could have one afternoon together that didn't end in a fight, couldn't they? Maybe it was a fantasy, but if anyone deserved a break from harsh reality right now, it was her. Why not pretend, for a little while, that everything was as fine and happy as she used to fantasize it could be.

Casey had just cut the head off the largest fish when the back door opened and Mary Elisabeth stepped out. "Hey there," she called, and headed toward the picnic table where he was working. She'd taken off the dish towel apron and held an oversized pair of pliers out in front of her like a bridal bouquet. "I thought maybe these would help," she said, stopping beside him.

"Yeah, thanks." He took the pliers, trying to remember what he was supposed to do with them.

"The easiest way is to use the pliers to pull the skin back, and sort of turn it inside out." She smiled, and tucked her hair behind one ear. She had about five earrings in each ear, a row of sparkling stones curving up from the lobe.

"Right. I remember now." He gripped the leathery fish skin with the pliers and tugged it back, aware of the muscles in his arms bulging with the effort. He'd taken off his shirt to keep from getting it dirty, and because it was hot out. He hoped she didn't think he looked like a pale, skinny kid.

"Hey, you're pretty strong." When she wrapped her hand around his bicep and squeezed, he almost dropped the pliers, but managed to hang onto them and the slippery fish.

"Thanks," he choked out, and tossed the now-naked fish into the dishpan. Sadie sat next to the table, eyes focused hopefully on the pan.

"How's the pup working out?" Mary Elisabeth raked her long nails through Sadie's hair. The dog half closed her eyes and swept the dirt with her tail. "Del said your mom wasn't too happy about him bringing her over."

"Aw, she's pretty much over that now. Sadie's a great dog."

She smiled at him again, and it was as if someone

had turned the sun's heat up a notch all of a sudden. He could feel sweat running down the small of his back. He started on the next fish and she moved closer. She wasn't wearing a bra and her nipples showed through the thin material of the tank top. He had to force his gaze back on the fish, or risk cutting his thumb off. "Not bad for a Yankee boy," she said as he stripped the second fish.

"I'm not a Yankee." *Or a boy*, he wanted to add, but of course to her he was. How old was she anyway? Probably twenty-five or so, at least.

"My daddy always said anybody who lived north of Amarillo was a Yankee to him." She laughed and climbed up onto the table and sat facing him, her feet on the bench. The muddy scent of catfish mingled with the sweet flower smell of her perfume.

He didn't know what to think of her. Was she flirting with him, or was she just one of those women who flirted with everybody? He tossed a third fish into the dishpan. Probably the latter. It wasn't like she'd be interested in him or anything.

"So how did you meet my my uncle Del?" he asked.

"He came into the water department to pay an overdue bill. While I was processing the paperwork, he started telling these really corny jokes. Like, what weighs five thousand pounds and wears glass slippers?"

"Um, I don't know."

"Cinderelephant! Or, what's large and gray and goes

around and around in circles? An elephant stuck in a revolving door."

"And you thought this was funny?"

She laughed. "They were so silly. And he had such a funny look on his face when he told them. He had us all in stitches. There's nothing a woman likes better than a man who can make her laugh."

He filed this away for future reference, though he wasn't sure how many women would be wowed by elephant jokes. "So that's what the big attraction is between you two—the fact that he makes you laugh?"

"Del is a man who doesn't let others' expectations interfere with his happiness. He's carefree, and I admire that."

He tossed a fish into the dishpan and picked up the knife again. "Mom says he's irresponsible." She said that about Casey, too, and she had the same sour look on her face when she said it. But Mary Elisabeth didn't make it sound like such a bad thing.

She sighed. "Yeah, sometimes he is. But you have to take the bad with the good with people, you know?"

A loud, trilling sounded nearby, accompanied by the flutter of wings. They looked up, and Casey spotted the flash of red and black on the end of a branch of the pine tree overhead. "Cardinal," he said.

"Does everybody in your family watch birds?"

He turned back to the fish he was filleting. "Not really. But Grandpa is teaching me some things."

She looked toward the house, her expression sad. "It must be hard for him, not being able to talk or move very easy."

"Yeah, I imagine it's no fun."

"I mean, it must be worse for someone like him. He's spent his whole life watching creatures that can fly." She looked up again, her head thrown back, neck arched, emphasizing the smooth hollow of her throat. "Birds must be about the freest things in the world, and there he is stuck in a crippled-up body."

The tenderness of her words surprised him. Why would she care about his grandfather, a man she didn't even know? And why would someone who could be so poetic about birds be hanging out with his uncle Del? He couldn't figure this chick out.

He tossed the last fillet in the dishpan. "They're done."

"You did a great job." She hopped off the table and picked up the dishpan. "Thanks." She walked back to the house, hips swaying. He watched her go, feelings stirring up in him like sand on a creek bottom.

Sixteen was about the most miserable age to be, he decided. He was too young to do anything about his out-and-out lust for his uncle's girlfriend, and too old to pretend such feelings didn't exist. He was too young to be truly on his own, and too old to be happy spending the summer with his sick old grandfather and his mom, who acted as if she'd forgotten how to smile.

Going back to Denver wasn't an option; he'd feel guilty for deserting his mom, and once there he'd end up fighting with his dad anyway.

He was screwed no matter what he did. He'd spent a lot of time looking for a way to make things better, but he couldn't get around that one truth: right now, it sucked to be him.

They sat down to dinner just before sunset. The table was heaped with bowls and platters and baskets of food—coleslaw, sliced tomatoes, fried potatoes and hush puppies. Mary Elisabeth had knocked herself out making a feast, and hardly broken a sweat doing it.

Karen watched the young woman with the dispassion of an anthropologist. Mary Elisabeth really was too good to be true. She'd insisted on sitting next to Martin and helping him, "So we can get to know each other better." He could maneuver a fork fairly well with his right hand, but once the food was in his mouth, it didn't always stay. And he tended to choke, so small pieces and a reminder to chew thoroughly were important.

"You're doing real good, Mr. Engel," Mary Elisabeth said cheerfully, deftly wiping the corners of his mouth with a damp dish towel. When Karen talked to him like this, he glared at her, as if he realized just how patronizing she was being. But with Mary Elisabeth, he looked almost happy. Even seventy-year-old curmudgeons weren't immune to the appeal of a sexy young girl.

So what was she doing with Del? And why should Karen care? Frankly, her brother deserved to have someone take advantage of him, the way he'd taken advantage of so many others.

"Casey tells me you've been teaching him about birds," Mary Elisabeth said as she laid another piece of fish on Martin's plate and cut it into tiny pieces. "I ought to have you teach me some. I only know the common ones around here, like cardinals and blue jays."

Her breasts in the thin tank top jiggled as she sliced into the fish. Karen wondered if her father appreciated the show. Probably. After all, he was male and breathing.

The girl would be easy to dislike, if nothing else because she was Del's floozy of the moment. But Mary Elisabeth was too genuine and just plain nice not to feel friendly toward. And the fact that she took so much time with Martin—more time than his own son—had landed her a permanent soft spot in Karen's heart.

"You want another hush puppy? Here's one that's not too greasy." She offered up the morsel of fried cornbread and Martin opened his mouth like a baby bird.

He chewed and chewed, mouth contorted. Karen looked away. It really wasn't a pretty sight.

"Guh. Guh!"

"Did you hear that?" Mary Elisabeth dropped her fork and beamed at them. "He said 'good.'"

"Didn't sound like anything to me." Del speared a slice of tomato and added it to his plate.

"No, he said 'good.' I know he did." She looked at Karen. "You heard it, didn't you?"

"I heard something." She studied her father. "Can you say it again?" she asked.

He worked his mouth, but nothing came out. His eyes sparked with frustration, and he shook his head.

Mary Elisabeth patted his arm. "That's okay. We know you said it. It's a start. It means the parts of your brain in charge of talking are starting to wake up."

Karen was skeptical of this unscientific explanation, but her father seemed placated by it. He picked up his fork and focused on eating again.

Del turned to Casey. "What's new with you, sport?" he asked.

"I got an e-mail from Matt this afternoon," Casey said. "He said to tell everybody hello."

"Oh? What's he up to?" Karen asked. The only time she heard from Matt these days was when *she* called *him*. It hurt to think he'd contacted his brother and not her.

"Dad's made him foreman on some job at a hospital or something. He and Audra had a big fight and broke up, but I'm guessing they'll get back together. They always do."

"He didn't say anything about any trouble with Audra when I talked to him two days ago." She stabbed at a piece of fish. "What happened?"

Casey shrugged. "I dunno. I guess they split about a week or so ago, so it was old news."

Old news to everyone but her. She tried to hide her hurt behind motherly concern. "I hope he's not too upset," Karen said. "He's awfully young to be getting serious about anyone."

"He's older than you were when you married Dad," Casey pointed out.

She flushed. "Girls are different. They mature faster. Not to mention I was too young, too. I just got lucky with your father." She'd been happy with Tom, but she couldn't help wondering what her life would have been like if she hadn't met him when she did. Would she have stayed in Tipton, married a local man and had a different kind of life? A life more like Tammy's? Or would she have found some other way to leave home, and distanced herself even further from her family?

"I think it's romantic when two people find each other when they're young and then spend the rest of their lives together," Mary Elisabeth said. "But I'm glad I didn't settle down too early."

"I hope you don't have any ideas about settling down now." Del opened a fresh beer. "Because I've spent way too much time tied down. I'm ready to cut loose."

Mary Elisabeth smiled, a Mona Lisa smirk. "No, I've still got a lot of things I want to do. I'd like to travel some, and see more of the world."

"I took you to Corpus Christi just last month." Del

winked at the rest of them to let them in on the joke. "Ain't that enough traveling for you?"

"Not by half, big guy." She swatted his hand. "You'd better be nice to me and maybe when I decide to start my travels, I'll take you with me."

"I'm glad you haven't left just yet." Casey swabbed a potato through a pool of ketchup. "I bet Matt and Dad wish they were here right now, eating all this great food." He grinned at Del. "You sure lucked out, finding a girlfriend who could cook so good."

"Aren't you sweet." Mary Elisabeth reached over to take a swig from Del's beer, her own long since empty.

"Guh! Guh!" Her father's fork clattered against his plate and he glared at them, as if defying them to deny that he had, indeed, spoken.

"It *is* good." Karen reached across the table and took his hand in hers. He gripped her fingers tightly, his skin cool and papery. The gesture brought tears to her eyes, and she rapidly blinked them away. "You're making progress," she said. "You're going to get better."

How much better would things get between them, though? He responded more to Mary Elisabeth, a woman he'd just met, than he ever had to her. Was she wasting her time trying to look after him, while her oldest son and her husband went on with their lives without her? How long could she stay away before they began to think they didn't need her at all?

What would she do with herself if the day ever came when she really wasn't needed? When she had only herself to answer to?

CHAPTER 8

*I am no bird; and no net ensnares me; I am a free
human being with an independent will...*
—*Charlotte Brontë*, Jane Eyre

Walking through the gates at Mitchell Speedway
the following Saturday was like stumbling across some
relic in an attic trunk and being reminded of a part of
life long since forgotten. Karen hadn't thought of this
place in twenty-five years, yet it had once been one of
the social centers of her universe. How many Friday
and Saturday nights in spring and summer had she
spent avoiding splinters on the wooden bleachers, or
lined up along the chain link fence breathing the sweet
smell of high-octane fuel and lusting after the drivers
who, more often than not, were more in love with car-
buretors and fuel cells than they ever would be with any
woman?

She followed Tammy and her children to the stands,
the warped boards rattling underfoot as they climbed
toward the middle, where they'd have the best view of

the track and the least risk of choking on dust and fumes. They filed into a row, Tammy's younger children, Jamie and April, climbing up one step to sit behind the women.

While Tammy distributed stadium chairs, binoculars and cold drinks, Karen looked out over the paved oval. "My God, this place hasn't changed at all," she said, staring at the Whitmore Tires sign that had graced the back wall of the track when she was a girl.

"They put in a new grandstand three years ago," Tammy said as she worked on redoing April's ponytail. "Stand still, baby."

Karen squinted at the white-painted grandstand across the way. "It looks the same to me."

"Well, you know there's a lot of tradition associated with racing. People like to uphold that."

In her high school days, it had been tradition for the drivers to carry hip flasks, from which they offered sips of whiskey to the girls who hung around after closing. Karen had drunk from her share of those flasks, and taken more than one wild ride around the track lit only by moonlight, her escort a not-entirely-sober racer, the car fishtailing around curves, engine smoking down the straightaway as the driver sought to impress her.

She shuddered at the memory. Had she ever really been that young and clueless? That reckless?

"Do you want some Fritos?" Tammy offered the open bag of chips. "There's dip, too."

She shook her head. "What time do the races start?"

"Seven o'clock. I always like to get here a little early in case Brady or the guys need anything."

"Can we go down to the pits now?" Jamie said.

They made their way down from the stands toward the pit area. The scent of oil and fuel stung Karen's nose and the throb of engines vibrated through her chest. They picked their way around stacks of tires and groups of men who huddled around cars. The men stood in groups of four and five, their heads and shoulders disappearing beneath the open hoods like lion tamers swallowed up by their charges. They passed several familiar faces—some whose names she remembered, others she couldn't recall. They all seemed to remember her, however. "Hey, Karen, how's it going?"

"Good to see you, Karen."

As if they'd last laid eyes on her yesterday instead of twenty or more years ago.

Brady was bent over under the hood of his car, fiddling with a wrench. He straightened when they approached. "I brought you a cold drink," Tammy says, handing him a Coke she'd snugged into a Koozie with the name of the local auto parts dealer emblazoned on the front. She looked past him, into the engine compartment. "Did you get the problem with the clutch fixed?"

"Yeah, finally. She's hooked up now." He grinned over at Karen. "There's this old boy, Darren Scott, he and I have been trading first place in the standings all spring. I'm determined to beat him tonight."

"There he is over there," April volunteered.

She turned and saw a man with graying brown hair and a goatee, standing beside a black-and-white car with the number nine painted on its side. "Cocky son-ovabitch," Brady said good-naturedly.

"April, don't forget you promised Sandra Wayne you'd watch little Seth for her," Tammy reminded her daughter.

"I hadn't forgotten." April scuffed the dirt with the toe of her tennis shoe. "I was just waiting to say good-bye to Daddy."

"You go on now, pumpkin." Brady leaned over and gave the girl a kiss. Karen felt a stab of longing as she watched them. Her father had never made such a casual gesture of affection.

"You should eat something," Tammy said to Brady. She smoothed the back of his flame-retardant suit. "You want me to bring you a corn dog or something after the race?"

"Nah, I'm okay. I'll probably go out with some of the guys for a few beers."

"All right, then." Tammy stood on tiptoe to kiss him on the lips. "Have a good race. We'll be cheering for you."

They made their way back to the bleachers. "It's amazing that Brady's still racing after all this time," Karen said.

"He did quit for a while, when the kids were little and we just flat didn't have the money. But he took it up again a few years back." She glanced at Karen.

"He says it keeps him young. I'm happy it keeps him out of trouble."

"What do you mean? Brady never struck me as the type to get into trouble." Even in school, Brady had been one of the straightest arrows they knew. Except for racing cars, he never did anything illegal, immoral or inconsistent.

"Well, there was this little secretary at work who was sniffing around him, but I got wind of it and put a stop to it." The determination in Tammy's voice and the hard line of her jaw made Karen look twice at her friend. Tammy always seemed so easygoing. Then again, it made sense that she'd be fierce when it came to protecting her family, and by extension, her marriage.

"You don't worry about all the groupies who hang out at the tracks?" Karen asked, remembering her own youthful indiscretions.

Tammy shook her head. "With me and all the kids here, he wouldn't have a chance to look at another woman. Besides, when he's here, all he's thinking about is his car. That thing is his baby."

"You're not jealous?" Her tone was light, teasing, but she was serious.

Tammy shook her head. "Nah. I'm the one he goes to bed with every night. I'm not worried about anything else."

They found their seats and settled in to watch the

first race. "Brady's in the second qualifying heat to-night," Tammy said.

Karen nodded, the racing lingo coming back to her. Groups of racers competed in the qualifying heat for post position in the main race, or feature. Brady raced stock cars, which started life as American-made street cars but were so highly modified now as to be unrecognizable as descendants of the family sedan.

The first heat was over almost before Karen knew it. Then it was Brady's turn. His bright red-and-white Chevrolet was easy to spot in the crowd, and he led the pack most of the way, crossing the finish line inches ahead of the next racer. "Oh, he'll be happy about that," Tammy said, grinning.

The qualifying heats out of the way, the track was prepped for the feature race. Karen amused herself watching the crowd. It was an eclectic audience, dominated by groups of men in cowboy hats or ball caps, jeans and T-shirts. There were a good number of families mixed in, the women carrying toddlers or babies on one hip, children playing tag and hide-and-seek beneath the glow of mercury vapor lights.

The teenagers segregated themselves in knots of five or six, the boys mostly separate from the girls, each group watching the other with a show of studied indifference.

She spotted one girl, probably sixteen or seventeen, her heavy makeup and teased hair a clue that she was trying to look older. She was standing with a pair of slightly older men—drivers or mechanics, judging by the shirts they wore that were plastered with the names of auto parts suppliers. The girl was smoking a cigarette. She laughed and threw her head back to blow the smoke out of her nose, while the men looked on admiringly.

Karen caught her breath, remembering herself at that age. For a brief period she, too, had taken up smoking, and carefully choreographed every gesture involved with the habit. Hold the cigarette like this. Tilt her head like that. This was how the cool people looked, how they acted. If she could get the moves right, she could be one of them. Someone better than herself.

Someone different than she'd turned out to be. Back then, she'd dreamed of having exciting adventures, passionate romances, visiting exotic places. She'd have laughed at the idea of settling for a staid life as a housewife and mother.

Is that what she'd done—settled for something less than her dreams? Had she taken the easy road, instead of the one she'd really wanted?

"Hey, Karen, you okay? What are you staring at?" Tammy's hand on her shoulder pulled her back to the present.

She shook her head. "Nothing. I'm fine."

"Are you sure? You've gone all white." Tammy shoved a Coke into Karen's hand. "You've been living in the mountains too long. You're not used to the heat." She turned to her son. "Jamie, wet a rag in that ice chest and wring it out for me."

"No, I'm fine." Karen tried unsuccessfully to fend off the wet towel, which Tammy draped around her neck.

"That'll help cool you off," Tammy said.

"Thanks." The damp chill did feel good in the lingering heat.

"I'll bet it's nice and cool in Denver right now," Tammy said, settling back in her seat once more.

"It does cool off a lot at night." Karen and Tom liked to take a drink onto their back deck after sunset, and sit in the growing darkness, talking. Mostly about work or the boys.

Rarely about things that mattered. The memory sent a pain through her chest, a sharp longing that stole her breath. What had she missed, by not making an effort to dig deeper?

To be more honest about her feelings and opinions, instead of always trying to smooth over any rough patches and disagreements.

"I'll bet you miss that." Tammy pulled a round cardboard fan from her bag and fluttered it back and forth under her chin. "I'd hate to live somewhere where it was cold in the winter, but summer does tend to drag on forever around here."

"Mama, I want a fan, too," Jamie whined.

"Here you go, honey." Tammy handed over her fan,

which Karen saw now was imprinted with the name of a local funeral parlor.

Karen remembered all the hours she'd spent placating Matt and Casey this way. Small children were so needy at times. It grew tiring, but now that they were more independent, a deep nostalgia for those times lingered in her. The boys had counted on her then, and she'd always been there for them.

Now that they were more independent and all but grown, she felt an emptiness, and a selfish longing for the old days when she'd been the center of their universe.

"They're getting ready to start." Tammy elbowed Karen and directed her attention to the track. As the green flag dropped, the cars surged forward in a cloud of exhaust. Karen found herself watching Tammy, instead of the cars on the track. She could judge the action by the expression on her friend's face. When Brady's car skidded through a turn, Tammy gasped and bit her knuckle, her shoulders sagging with relief as he righted the car in the straightaway. When a crash ahead of him forced him to brake and lurch the car to the right, she gave a muffled shriek and rose up from her seat, plopping down again when he was clear of danger.

As the cars neared the final lap, she bounced in her seat, hands pumping. "Come on, baby. Come on, baby. Come on," she muttered, faster and faster as the cars raced on.

When the checkered flag dropped and the results board showed Brady had come in second, Tammy squeezed her hands together and released a sigh. "Second is good," she said. "But Brady would be a lot happier with first."

"Mama, I'm hungry," Jamie said.

"Have some chips and dip. And there's some beef jerky in there, too." Tammy dispensed snacks, having easily transformed from cheering for her man to catering to her children. She was so calm and efficient.

A sense of familiarity overwhelmed Karen as she watched her friend. She recognized the urgency underlying the capable movements and precision organization. You had to hurry to stay on top of everyone's needs, your brain spinning at a frantic pace to keep up. Even the outward calm was part of the act. You could never look anything less than absolutely capable. After all, if you fell apart, think how many people you'd take down with you. People who depended on you.

Karen had been there. She'd done that and she'd gotten the T-shirt and the souvenir crown that identified her as the queen manager/mother/organizer/volunteer/et cetera, et cetera....

The problem was, all this activity didn't leave any chance to slow down or retreat from the constant busyness of life. Sometimes she suspected that was the whole point. Being perfect in all her roles as wife, mom and business partner left little time to question her own needs, or to see her own flaws.

The idea made her feel queasy.

"Brady likes to stay after the race to go over everything on the car and talk to the other drivers," Tammy said. "There's three more features on the program, but we won't necessarily stay to see them all, if that's okay with you."

"That's fine. We'll leave whenever you're ready." Not knowing the drivers or having followed their careers, the races were interesting, but not compelling.

"I've got to get a roast ready for the Crock-Pot when we get home, so we can take it over to Mama and Daddy's after church tomorrow," Tammy said as she repacked the cooler and gathered up trash.

"Do you have dinner with them every Sunday?" Karen asked.

"Just about. Mama and I take turns cooking, so it works out."

"You don't get tired of that? I mean, do you ever think about doing something different? Just for a change."

"Not really. Besides, my folks would be so disappointed if we didn't show. There'll be plenty of time for doing things differently when they're gone."

Tammy's words echoed in Karen's head as she followed her friend out of the stands and across the grounds toward the parking lot. At what age did you cross over from feeling as if there was always *plenty of time* to the sense that the hours and days were rushing away from you, like water through your fingers? Certainly some sense of urgency had brought her here to look after her father. She'd come expecting to learn more about him, to maybe even figure out what made him the way he was.

She hadn't counted on having to face so much of herself in the hours when she wasn't caring for him. It unnerved her to think she didn't always like the things she was finding out.

The day after her visit to the races, Karen called Tom. She needed to hear his voice, and to try to put into words the things she'd felt sitting there in the bleachers the night before. "Do you think I'm a martyr?" she asked once they got past the initial hellos.

"Do I think you're what?"

"Do you think I'm one of those women who are always rushing around doing things for other people and never looking after themselves? The kind of woman who always eats the heels of the bread because no one else in the family will, or who doesn't buy new shoes for herself because her kid wants new sneakers."

"I thought that was all part of being a mom," he said. "What brought this on?"

"I don't know. I went to the races with Tammy Wainwright last night. I was watching her with her husband and kids and I saw myself—so busy looking after other people, I couldn't look after myself."

An Important Message from the Editors

Dear Reader,

Because you've chosen to read one of our fine novels, we'd like to say "thank you"! And, as a special way to say thank you, we're offering to send you two more novels similar to the one you are currently reading, and a surprise gift – absolutely FREE!

Please enjoy the free books and gift with our compliments...

Pam Powers

Peel off Seal and Place Inside...

FREE GIFT SEAL

EDITOR'S ... THANK YOU

We'd like to send you two free books to introduce you to our new line – Harlequin® NEXT™! These novels by acclaimed, award winning authors are filled with stories about rediscovery and reconnection with what's important in women's lives. These are relationship novels about women redefining their dreams.

THERE'S THE LIFE YOU PLANNED. AND THERE'S WHAT COMES NEXT.

"I don't have a clue what you're talking about. But I can tell you I wish you were up here right now, looking after some of this paperwork. I'm drowning in it."

Was that her most important role in his life—personal secretary? "Isn't the temp working out?"

"She only works three days a week, and I spend as much time showing her what to do as I do on my own work."

Was that supposed to make her feel guilty for going out with her friend? "I'll be back before you know it. Dad's doing really well. He's started to say a few words. And Casey's been a big help to me."

"He could be a big help here, too, if he wanted to."

She could feel the tension between her temples, as if someone had fastened a band around her head and just twisted it tighter. She didn't know what to say to Tom. She couldn't say what he seemed to want to hear—that she would drop everything and run to help him. "We'll both be home as soon as we're able." Longing came back, sharp as a razor. "Maybe you can find some time to come down for a visit. Just for a weekend. I'd like that."

"Yeah. I'll try." He took a deep breath, switching gears. "So how were the races?"

"Good. Brady came in second."

"I can't believe he's still racing."

"Tammy says it keeps him out of trouble."

He laughed. "He should go into business for himself. He'll be too busy to get into trouble."

"How's Matt?"

"Great. I made him foreman on the Adventist Hospital job and he's doing terrific. I'm really proud of him."

"Casey said something about him breaking up with Audra."

"Oh, I think they split up for a few days, but he said something about going to the movies with her the other night, so I guess they're back together."

"You didn't ask?"

"It's none of my business."

Men! As far as she was concerned, everything that affected her son was her business, at least as long as he lived at home. Part of being a parent was caring about what happened to your children.

"Can I talk to him?" Maybe she could get him to tell her what had happened with Audra.

"He's not here right now. I'll tell him you called."

And he wouldn't call back. He was too busy—too much in his own world these days, which didn't have much room for his mom.

"Listen, I've got to go now," Tom said. "I'm meeting a client to go over a bid for a project."

"Think about getting away for a visit. You could use a break and it would be great to see you."

"I'll think about it."

He sounded sincere enough, but without facial cues it was difficult to tell if he was trying to placate her or he truly intended to fly down. Not for the first time, she wondered if being here with her father was worth the strain on her marriage. Why was she here, really? If it was just to nurse her dad back to health, she could hire someone to do that.

No, she'd come down here to try to build a relationship with her father, before it was too late. She wanted to learn about him—but also to learn about herself. She didn't want to go through life like someone else's servant, or a robot who was afraid to stop moving. Here was her chance to slow down, to reacquaint herself with the part of herself with whom she'd lost touch.

Karen was putting away laundry the following Wednesday when she found an old photo album in the hall closet. It was in a pile of miscellaneous pictures and envelopes full of old negatives that had fallen behind the stacks of sheets and towels. She pulled it out and opened it, the black paper pages brittle beneath her hands.

The first thing she saw was a picture of her eight-year-old self, dressed in cutoff jeans and a striped T-shirt, posing on a rock, one hand shielding her eyes as she stared off in the distance, a serious look on her face.

She laughed, and carried the album to the sofa. All the photos were from the family's vacation to Yellowstone that year. She smiled at a picture of the four of them posed in front of Old Faithful. Her father, of course, had binoculars around his neck. Del's lower lip was stuck out in a pout. She seemed to remember he was mad because his mother wouldn't let him throw rocks in the geyser.

And there was Karen, standing between her mother and father, a huge smile on her face. She looked so happy.

It had been a fun trip. While her father wandered off to look for birds, her mother took her and Del on a nature hike, bribing them with the promise of roasted marshmallows and hot dogs when they returned. They had climbed rocks, balanced on fallen logs and picked wildflowers, laughing and shrieking with the abandon of children who had spent three days cooped up in the backseat of a car.

Rounding a curve in the trail, they had come upon a grizzly sow feeding in some berry bushes. Sara had screamed and gathered the children about her. The bear had ignored them and lumbered off. Del started crying and Sara tried to comfort him, while Karen stared, fascinated, at the magnificent animal.

Back at camp, she had rushed to be the first to tell her father the news of the sighting. He'd helped her look up bears in one of his guidebooks and they'd read about grizzlies. Closing her eyes, she could still remember the feel of his arm around her as he held her close and turned the pages of the book, the smell of insect repellent and campfire smoke permeating his clothes.

How had she forgotten that moment? Why did she so seldom remember those things now, but rather focused on the disappointments of her youth?

Maybe because those happy times made all the other days seem that much worse. Those good memories were a reminder of what might have been—the ideal they approached, but never really reached.

She was still studying the photos, and remembering, when Sara arrived an hour later. She swept into the house bearing a tower of Tupperware containers. "Left-overs from my ladies club luncheon," she explained as she unpacked the containers onto a plate. "I thought you'd appreciate not having to cook."

Karen admired the array of chicken salad, fruit salad, salmon sandwiches cut in quarters, crusts removed and a container of vaguely familiar hors d'oeuvre-looking items.

"What are these?" she asked.

Sara made a face. "Sushi. California rolls, I think. They're from Estelle Watson. She fancies herself a *gourmet.*"

Karen sampled one of the rolls. "They're good."

Sara made a face. "I suppose. Though why good old deviled eggs or cocktail sausages aren't good enough for her I'll never know." She filled a plate with some of each of the dishes and handed it to Karen. "I'm betting you haven't had lunch yet. Eat."

"Yes, ma'am." Karen carried the plate to the table. Her mother followed and sat across from her.

"Where's Casey?" Sara asked.

"He and Sadie walked down the road to a neighbor's who has a pool."

"Who is Sadie?"

Karen flushed. "Sadie's a dog. A big mutt Del foisted off on us. Casey's crazy about her."

"And you didn't have the heart to tell him he couldn't keep her." Sara shook her head. "You spoil that boy."

"You're one to talk. You never said no to Del."

Sara smiled. "I see a lot of Del in Casey. I suppose there are worse things than having a dog. He might have asked for a motorcycle. Or a drum set." She spotted the photo album and slid it toward her. "What's this?"

"I found it in the linen closet this morning. It's pictures from our vacation to Yellowstone. Do you remember?"

Sara slipped on her reading glasses and opened the album. "Oh, I remember. The bear."

"That's right. We saw that grizzly bear when we were out hiking."

"I was so terrified after that I refused to spend another night in the tent."

"Is that why we moved to the lodge? I didn't think much about it, I was so excited to be able to swim in the pool."

"Children are easy to please at that age."

She ate in silence for a moment. She would never have described herself as *easy to please*. "What was I like as a child?" she asked after a moment.

"You were a very serious child. Frightfully solemn." Sara removed her glasses and closed the album. "I never knew quite what to make of you. You took after your father that way."

"I did?" She had never thought she had that much in common with her dad.

"Oh yes. Everything was so dreadfully important to you, from doing your homework perfectly to dressing just so. If anything went wrong, you would pout or cry." She shook her head. "Del was much easier. He and I knew how to have fun."

Her mother made her sound so…unlovable. "I wish we'd taken more vacations like the one to Yellowstone. That was fun."

"After your father saw all the 'easy' birds in the United States, he wanted to spend his free time abroad. The thought of traveling in remote areas with two children didn't appeal to me, so we stayed home."

"Didn't it bother you, that he wasn't more a part of our lives?"

"It did. And it didn't." She tilted her head, considering the question. "Sometimes it was easier being able to do things my own way, without interference. And men weren't expected to be as involved with their children back then. That was the mother's job."

Karen ate another California roll. "Is that why you waited until we were grown to divorce him?"

"Partly. I don't know if it's hormones, or empty

nest, or an awareness of time getting away, but a lot of women in their forties get restless. They start looking for more in life."

"I thought it was men who had the midlife crises."

"I'm not talking crises. It could be something as simple as changing the way you wear your hair or taking up a new hobby." She smiled. "It's a wonderful chance to find out what you're really capable of."

"How old were you when you did all this?"

Sara gave Karen a knowing look. "About the age you are now, I think. Isn't that interesting?"

She looked away. Interesting. And a little unnerving. She had enough changes going on in her life right now without contemplating more. And yet the idea of making some kind of choice for her life, instead of always reacting to whatever was thrown at her, held a powerful appeal.

Did she want things to keep moving along the way they always had been, or was she ready to make some changes? And what kind of changes? She didn't know any other kind of life than the one she'd lived for years as a wife and mother and business partner. There had to be other options out there, but the thought of exploring them stole her breath. Reaching for something new seemed to mean letting go of something old. What if she released the wrong thing, and ended up worse off than before?

CHAPTER 9

It's not only fine feathers that make fine birds.
—Aesop, *"The Jay and the Peacock"*

The Great Crested Flycatcher perched on the uppermost limb of the big pine. The compact silhouette gave it away as a flycatcher; Martin had thought it an Ash-throated at first. Then it turned and sunlight highlighted the yellow belly and the distinctive crest.

He glanced at Karen. She was studying the tree intently but had yet to spot the bird. She was looking too low down. He leaned over and tugged at her sleeve, then pointed toward the top of the tree. "Look."

It came out to his ears more like *oog* but she seemed to understand, and elevated her gaze.

"I see it!" Her voice held the excitement of a child spying a prize at an Easter egg hunt. She fumbled with the binoculars, sighting through them, then scanning the treetop, struggling to locate the bird again.

Did she remember nothing he'd taught her? He grunted to get her attention, then demonstrated the proper technique. First, find the bird with the naked eye. Then, without looking away from the bird, lift the binoculars into place and adjust the focus.

The flycatcher leaped into view, the gray throat, yellow belly and rufous tail feathers making identification easy.

"I see it now, but what is it?" Karen asked.

He lowered the binoculars and gestured toward the field guide at her elbow. It wasn't going to do her any good if he identified everything for her.

She picked up the guide and flipped through it, glancing from time to time at the bird, which remained still on the perch, as if posing for them.

Martin wondered sometimes if birds knew they were being watched. It was a frivolous idea, and he was not a frivolous man, but too many times when he'd been unsure about an identification, the bird in question had turned to show some singular marking that answered his question. It made him wonder....

"Is it some kind of vireo? No, that's not right." She flipped through the guidebook, studying the pictures, scanning through the list of identifying features, habitat maps and descriptions of birdcalls. "A flycatcher then. The size is right." She looked at him for confirmation and he nodded.

"All right, then. I can eliminate the ones that don't live here." She hurriedly flipped pages, impatient as she narrowed in on identifying the sighting. "That one's head isn't right.... That one doesn't live here.... That one's wrong...." She stopped and studied the illustration of the Great Crested Flycatcher, then checked the bird above them through the binoculars again.

Obliging of it to sit still so long, Martin thought. Most of the time in the field you were lucky to catch more than a passing glimpse. He'd have to teach her to make a more rapid assessment. She needed to learn to note features such as the presence or lack of wing bars, the shape of the beak, colors and their pattern, eye stripes or rings, and a dozen other distinguishing characteristics, all in a matter of seconds.

He'd long felt that birders would make excellent witnesses in the event of a crime, provided they were focused on the villain, and not some more interesting feathered quarry on a nearby telephone wire.

"It's this one." She held the book out in front of him and pointed to the painting of the Great Crested Flycatcher.

He nodded and waved a shaking hand toward the notebook in her lap. "Mark." Which came out *mar* but she understood.

She carefully noted the time, day and location of the sighting. "That's three new ones this afternoon," she said. "I'm afraid I have a long way to go to catch up to you."

She never would catch up, of course. She had no serious interest in being a big lister. Which suited him. He hadn't worked this hard to make records that would be easily broken, even by his own progeny.

It was enough that she wanted to sit here with him now, to learn a little of what he had to pass on to her. She'd surprised him when she'd come to his office a few days ago and asked him to teach her about birding. For forty years she'd shown little interest in his avocation, and now that he had lost most of his mobility and practically all his powers of speech, she wanted to share this with him.

"I just thought, as long as I was here, it would be a good time to take up a new hobby," she'd said.

A more morbid man might have suspected she wanted to learn his secrets before he carried them to the grave with him.

"It's very peaceful here, isn't it?" she said, focusing on the tree once more. It rose thirty feet into the air and in its branches Martin could hear and see dozens of birds, mostly the chickadees, nuthatches, titmice and sparrows common to backyard feeders throughout the United States. Bright red Northern Cardinals and blue-and-white Eastern Jays rounded out the local hoi polloi. Karen had added all these to her list in the first two days of their birding together.

She'd impressed him with her ability to sit quiet and still, observing. Before, she'd struck him as a woman plagued with the need to be busy, like her mother, who had once protested that fidgeting had been proven to burn calories, so she saw no need to give it up.

Maturity had brought a settledness to Karen he appreciated. Maybe she did have some qualities from his side of the genetic helix.

"Is that what attracted you to birding? This sort of zen quality to it?"

There was nothing zen about the compulsion he felt to list birds. It was as if the more time he spent finding birds and adding them to his list, the greater his chances of understanding their ethereal nature. Plus, he wanted to accomplish something few men had accomplished. Not blessed with great brains, brawn or ability, he'd sought to see more birds than anyone else in the world.

But he had no way of expressing this so that Karen would understand. Instead, he shrugged, and scanned the tree once more. Silence settled between them again, a stillness void of the awkwardness he'd felt too often in her presence. Birding had given them that, at least. Something they could do together without the need for conversation.

Except that Karen was in the mood to talk. "Do you remember when I was a little girl and you taught me about birds?" she asked.

He would not have called his few attempts to share his passion with his children a success. They grew impatient with sitting still so long, though Karen, at least, had had a good memory for names and details. He nodded.

"I think I probably spent more time picking wild-flowers and collecting pretty stones that I did actually seeing birds on our expeditions." She lowered the bin-oculars and turned to him. "Mostly what I enjoyed was getting to spend time alone with you."

He blinked, startled that she had such positive memories of what, for him, had been frustrating outings. The boundless energy and short attention span of his children when they were small overwhelmed him, and he had never felt he was really getting through to them.

"I found a photo album the other day, with pictures from that vacation we took to Yellowstone, when I was eight. Do you remember?"

He nodded. He'd seen Trumpeter Swans and Whooping Cranes during that trip, and Sara had been frightened by a bear. He also remembered that Karen had not been afraid at all. She'd been eager to tell him about the grizzly. Together, they'd looked through one of his nature guides, and read about the great bears. He had a sudden memory of eight-year-old Karen standing in the circle of his arms, listening raptly as he read to her from the guidebook. The realization that he had had a part in creating something as perfect and precious as this child had overwhelmed him. Affection and wonder and pride left him speechless, and terrified that he might do or say the wrong thing and lose her alto-gether. When Sara called Karen to wash up for supper he was almost relieved to have the chance to school his feelings into a more comfortable reserve.

He studied the woman beside him, looking for signs of that girl. They were there, in the dimple to the left of her mouth, and in the way she tilted her head to one side and smiled at him now. "That was a fun trip, wasn't it, Dad? I wish we'd taken more like that."

He nodded, and blinked away stinging tears. Regrets were a poison he wanted no part of, but now, speechless and immobile, they worked on him with painful intensity.

He grabbed up his own binoculars and raised them to his eyes, pretending to search the treetops once more. He was almost grateful he'd been robbed of the ability to speak. In the best of times, he'd never known what to say to his daughter. There were no words to explain this paradox of wanting to reclaim a closeness he had forfeited long ago, and the fear that the price he owed for such a privilege was far too dear.

Karen had turned to birding as a way to connect with her father, but she was surprised by how much she enjoyed looking for birds, watching their behavior and trying to determine their identity. She had no desire to count and categorize species the way her father did, but the solitary, out-of-doors nature of the activity made for a lot of time to be alone with her thoughts.

Her life up till now hadn't had much room for contemplation, and the nature of some of her thoughts surprised her. There was the usual litany of worries about

the boys, Tom, their landscaping business and her
father's health. But once she'd gotten all that out of the
way, she found herself remembering things that hadn't
come to mind in years—ambitions she'd had as a girl,
old hurts and triumphs long since put aside, beliefs
she'd held that hadn't proved true. In those hours spent
on the front porch or out back by the pond, eyes trained
overhead and heart turned inward, she felt like an ar-
chaeologist removing layers of refuse and artifacts to
reveal clues about her life as it was once lived, secrets
she'd once told herself and then forgotten.

She was sitting in a lawn chair by the pond,
watching a Golden-fronted Woodpecker trace a
crooked spiral up the trunk of a half-dead yellow pine
when Casey found her one late afternoon. Sadie ran
ahead to greet her, tail wagging. Karen ignored the dog
and jumped up from the chair. "What is it? Is Grandpa
okay?"

"He's okay. He's taking a nap." Casey bent and
scooped up a pine cone and hurled it toward the pond.
"I came out here to see what you were doing."

"Bird-watching." She held up the binoculars, feeling
a little foolish as she did so. To a teenager, watching
birds must seem about the most uncool thing a person
could do. "I'm trying to figure out what your grandfather finds so fascinating about it."

She sat once more and Sadie sat next to her and put
her head on Karen's knee. Karen absently rubbed her

ears and was rewarded with a steady drumming of the dog's tail. It amazed her how quickly the dog had insinuated herself into their lives. How quickly she'd come to seem, even to Karen, like part of the family.

"What have you seen so far?" Casey came to stand beside her chair.

She flipped to the front of the guidebook, where she'd been keeping her list. "This afternoon I've seen an Eastern Wood Pewee, two Killdeer and a Golden-fronted Woodpecker. Others, too, but those are the ones that are new to my list."

He sat on the ground beside her chair, long legs folded up like a grasshopper, knees sticking up. When was the kid going to stop growing? He'd need all new pants before school this fall. She frowned at a hole in the toe of his right shoe. "Why is there a hole in your shoe?"

He stretched out his leg and examined the hole. "I guess my toe rubbed through. These shoes are a little tight."

"We'll try to get you another pair one day this week." She added it to her mental list of things to do. Later, she'd transfer it to the running tally she kept in a notebook in her purse. *Her brain* she'd jokingly dubbed the notebook. The thing that enabled her to keep all her plates in the air.

"That'd be good." He gazed out over the small pond, silent for a moment, then said, "When we were little,

Grandpa would bring us out here after supper to fish. He'd put worms on our hooks and we'd toss our lines in, and while we waited for the fish to bite, he'd teach us about birds."

"He would?" She searched her brain for some memory of such a tender familial scene and found none. "I don't remember him spending that much time with y'all."

Casey scratched at a mosquito bite on his arm, then leaned back, propping his weight on his hands. "It was that summer I was nine. Matt and I stayed here with Grandpa and Grandma while you and Dad went on that cruise."

How could she have forgotten? It was the first vacation she and Tom had taken together since the boys were born. They'd spent a week in the Caribbean, drinking fruity drinks, soaking up the sun and making love every afternoon in their tiny cabin. They'd dubbed it their second honeymoon, and vowed to make it a semiannual tradition. But they'd never found the time or money to go again.

Sadness washed over her at that thought. Why had they denied themselves that chance at closeness, that opportunity to remember what made them a couple? If nothing else, this time spent apart had opened her eyes to all the little things they'd left out of their relationship, things maybe they both needed.

"So do you think Grandpa decided to be a petroleum engineer so he could travel all over looking for birds, or he started watching birds because his job took him all over the world?" Casey glanced up at her.

"The former, I think. I seem to remember he started birding while he was still in high school." She looked down at her son, at the cowlick at the top of his head. It delighted her that all the carefully applied styling gel in the world couldn't tame that little-boy curl of hair. "I guess he was lucky to find a job that allowed him to indulge his passion."

"I think it's cool when you can earn money and still do what you love." He plucked a piece of grass and twirled it between his fingers. "Like Uncle Del. He owns the oil-change shop, but he takes off whenever he wants to go fishing and stuff."

She struggled not to let her dismay show. Her brother as role model was not an idea that had ever crossed her mind. "Casey, look at me," she said.

He turned his head to her. The end of his nose was peeling with sunburn, and blond peach fuzz showed on his upper lip. She supposed he'd be shaving every day soon. She didn't know if she was ready to admit how much of a man he'd become.

"Your uncle Del can be a really nice guy," she said slowly, wary of painting her brother too black and therefore making him that much more attractive to a teenager. "But he hasn't always made the best choices in his life. Financial or personal."

"Well, yeah, but he's got a great girlfriend now, and

a cool truck." He looked at her sideways. "A fancy house isn't everything, you know."

She stifled a groan of aggravation. Of course a sixteen-year-old would think a great girlfriend and a cool truck were the height of personal success, but could she help it if she'd hoped for a little better perspective from her son?

"I'm not saying a fancy house is everything. And neither is a girlfriend and a truck. What's important is to spend some time right now, before you have to make choices, deciding what you want to do with your life. If you start on the right path when you're young, you'll save yourself a lot of grief."

She said the words with only a twinge of guilt. What did she know about choosing the right path? Almost nothing she'd set out to do in life had turned out quite as she'd imagined, from her choice of vocation, to the kind of marriage she'd have, to the relationship she'd have with her parents and her children. She was over forty and still trying to get things right. Who was she to preach to Casey, except a mother who hoped he'd do better at figuring things out than she had?

He tossed the blade of grass to the side and plucked another one, and began tearing it into tinier and tinier pieces. "Yeah, that's what everybody says, but really, what's so wrong with making mistakes? You learn things that way."

"But you aren't the only one your mistakes affect."

He dusted his hands together and stood. "You don't

have to worry about me. I'm not going to end up a bum. But if I did, at least I'd be a happy bum."

She made a face. "Those aren't exactly comforting words to a mother's ears."

He picked up the binoculars she'd dropped and focused them on the pond. "Parents worry too much."

"Children don't worry enough." She studied him, seeing Tom in the strong curve of his jaw and the fullness of his bottom lip. But she was there in his face, too, in the narrow nose and high forehead. She wanted so much for him—money, love, good health and freedom from worries. But most of all, she wanted him to be happy. "Isn't there anything you've thought about doing for a living? Anything that interests you?"

He lowered the binoculars. "I think I might like to be a writer."

"A novelist?"

He shrugged. "Maybe movies or plays. Or nonfiction stuff. Articles. Things like that. But I'd like to travel around some first, you know, to gather material."

She had a sudden recollection of a summer day when she and Tammy were working on their tans on a bluff overlooking the Trinity River. They'd been sharing deep thoughts and Karen had suddenly announced that after graduation, she was going to join the Peace Corps and work helping people in Africa. Where this sudden burst of altruism had come from, she couldn't have said, and after a few months, her noble ideals had died a quiet death. She'd gone to work for the hospital, met Tom, and so the rest of her life had played out.

But what would have happened if she'd held on to that impulse? How might her life have been different? She stood and put her arm around her son. "I think you'd make a great writer."

He flushed. "You do?"

"I do. You're smart and you have a good heart." Important things to remember when worry got the best of her. Maybe those things didn't add up to the kind of success she always envisioned for her children, but they surely couldn't hurt.

As for the mistakes she'd made, who was to say any of her other options would have turned out any better? It was nice to imagine she could have been a world traveler or a great humanitarian or a more devoted daughter or more passionate wife, but would any of those things really have made her any happier?

Was the answer, instead, to appreciate more what she had, or to reimagine her fantasies to closer fit her reality? Like the good memories of her childhood she was only beginning to unearth, maybe there was more to her life than she thought. Maybe the restlessness she was feeling now was only the beginning of discovering she was better off than she'd imagined.

Mary Elisabeth agreed to sit with Martin one afternoon so that Karen could take Casey to buy new shoes.

No one consulted Martin about the arrangement; Karen presented it to him as a *fait accompli*. He said nothing about it one way or another. It was a sad thing when a grown man had to have a babysitter.

But he could do worse than this young woman. Whatever else he could say about Del, he couldn't fault his taste in women. This one was designed to make a man think about sex, from her thick-lashed dark eyes to the fall of brown curls around her shoulders to the breasts that swelled her too-small T-shirt to the tight round bottom scarcely covered by her cutoffs.

She wore too much mascara and a ring in her navel, and he'd caught a glimpse of a butterfly tattooed over her left breast. In his younger years she'd have been deemed *fast* but he supposed nowadays she was just a normal young woman. They didn't try to pretend these days that they weren't as interested in sex as men always had been. There was something to be said for that kind of honesty.

Just as well she couldn't read the thoughts in his mind. It would probably shock her to know a man his age still contemplated such things. To her he was merely a dried-up husk in this wheelchair, incoherent and harmless.

Not that she'd have anything to fear from him even in his prime. He'd always been a man more inclined to thought than action, at least when it came to women. And he had enough dignity left not to make a fool of himself over a woman young enough to be his granddaughter.

"I thought maybe we could listen to some music," she said, looking through the bookshelves in his bedroom. He'd managed to get himself out of the bed and into his chair before she'd arrived, but he hadn't yet made it into his office when she swept in on a cloud of floral perfume. She flipped through the stacks of cassettes, then looked back at him, eyes wide. "These are all bird-calls."

He nodded. He would have liked to explain how he used the tapes to lure birds to him, but complex sentences were beyond his powers of speech at the moment.

"I guess you use these to learn all the different calls." She straightened and looked at hím. "I'm here to keep you company, so what would *you* like to do?"

"Office." The word came out slurred, so he tried again, concentrating on shaping his tongue to make the correct sounds. "Of-fice!"

"Karen said you like to spend a lot of time in your office." She took hold of the wheelchair and maneuvered him through the door and down the hall. The dog joined them, tail wagging, tongue lolling. Apparently Del had talked Karen into taking in the animal. Martin had never approved of dogs in the house, but as with everything else in his life these days, he had little say about it.

"Is over here by the desk all right?" Mary Elisabeth asked, parking the chair in front of the computer.

He nodded, and shifted onto his left hip. He'd lost weight and sometimes it felt as if his backbone was trying to poke through his skin. Mary Elisabeth noticed him fidgeting, and worry lines formed on her perfect forehead. "You need a pillow at the small of your back." She plucked a small pillow from the love seat by the window and arranged it behind his back. "And if you raise this footrest just a little..." She bent and adjusted the footrests, then straightened. "That will help take some of the pressure off your spine."

Skeptical, he settled back in the chair, but found that he was, indeed, more comfortable. He looked at her. "How?" How had she known this?

"Oh, my mom was in a wheelchair."

"Why?"

"She had MS. Multiple sclerosis. I can hardly remember when she wasn't in a wheelchair."

"Hard." Hard on a kid to have a parent who was crippled that way.

"Yeah, it was hard sometimes. I used to wish she was more like other kids' moms, until I figured out they all had problems, too." She shrugged. "Life is what it is. You have to make the best of it."

It was the kind of trite advice that usually annoyed him, but coming from her, it had the ring of truth. He studied her again. Her hair was pulled back from her face with tiny clips shaped like butterflies, and she wore half a dozen rings in each ear. When she smiled, dimples formed on either side of her mouth. No one looking at her would ever guess she was anything but carefree, even frivolous. "Your mom...alive?" he asked.

She shook her head. "She died when I was sixteen."

Too young. "Casey's...sixteen."

"Yeah. Kind of a tough age for a kid. You're trying to figure things out."

Plenty of people spent most of their lives trying to figure things out. For instance, he couldn't figure out why he'd been felled by a stroke in the prime of his birding career, or why his children too often seemed like strangers to him. Del hardly spoke to him, and Karen's words didn't always match the expression in her eyes. All his years spent observing wildlife around the globe hadn't prepared him for dealing with his adult children. When they were small, he'd told himself he'd be able to relate to them better as adults. They'd be more like peers, less dependent on him, less needy.

Yet now they accosted him with a whole different set of demands, still bound to him by blood and obligation, expecting to be treated as more than peers, needing him in a different way than they had as children, but seemingly needing him no less.

His eyes met Mary Elisabeth's. "Miss her?" He meant her mother.

"I do. It sneaks up on me sometimes. I'll be doing something and I'll wonder what she would have said or thought, or I wish she was with me. But I knew for a long time before she died that she probably wouldn't be around to see me grow up. It was hard, but it also made me appreciate the time we did have."

"Life…short." Her mother's life, but so many others, too. And the older you grew, the shorter your life ahead became. He had never contemplated such things before his stroke; now there were days when such thoughts blotted out everything else.

"It's a cliché, but true." She took hold of his hand and held it in hers. She had cool fingers with neatly manicured nails, painted shell-pink. "Enough morbid talk. You're going to be around a long time yet. And your talking is getting better. I don't have any trouble understanding you now."

She understood a great deal. Lessons some people never learned.

"So tell me about your bird-watching. I see all these awards on the walls." She turned to look at the plaques. "But why do you do it? Is it that you just like birds, or is there more to it?"

Yes, there was more to it. The fact that she got *that* made her rise another notch in his opinion. He wrinkled his face, trying to think how to explain. But his limited powers of speech failed him. He turned to the computer and typed.

Birding is a challenge. Something I can do others can't.

She nodded. "Like people who climb mountains or run marathons, or things like that."

Yes. But it is about the birds, too. They fascinate me.

"They are fascinating. And there are so many of them. Always more to discover." She turned her attention to the map that bristled with pins marking all the places he'd recorded bird sightings. "Look at all the places you've traveled. All the countries you've seen." She smiled over her shoulder at him. "I'd love to travel that way—to see all kinds of people and cultures."

He didn't tell her he'd spent most of his time in those countries away from people, searching for birds. Other than those he associated with through his work, he hadn't gotten to know the natives of the countries he'd visited.

Except one time.

Perhaps it was being here with Mary Elisabeth that brought the memory back to him, sharp and bright. He'd been in Thailand, ostensibly to do research for his employer, but he'd made sure to allow time on either end of the business trip to look for birds. At the airport alone he'd added three new birds to his life list.

A meeting had ended early and he'd gone to the beach near his hotel, thinking he might find a few shore birds to add to his list, bringing the total to 2,027.

He had found no birds, but had met a young woman. She was Polynesian, but she spoke softly accented

English. She had approached him, and struck up a casual conversation. He'd decided she was a prostitute, but didn't discourage her company.

He had ended up spending the evening and the night with her. She had been like Mary Elisabeth, with much more depth than her appearance had led him to expect. They talked about everything—nature, politics, books, life. Sitting with her he'd felt something come alive inside him. She had awakened him to things that might be missing in his life.

He'd returned home later in the week determined to pay more attention to those around him. The possibilities had excited him. But it was too late. His attempts to connect with his wife and children were met with indifference. He had waited too long and they had learned to live without him. Rather than try to overcome their resistance, he had slipped back into his old ways, focusing on his work and his lists of birds, self-contained and unemotional.

He was like a man who had stood by a campfire and enjoyed its warmth, but when the fire had died down, he'd been content to sit in the coolness. The warmth had been nice, but maybe it wasn't for him.

"What should we do now?" Mary Elisabeth perched on the corner of the desk.

"Music." He clicked the appropriate icon on the desktop and a Haydn concerto swelled from the speakers. It was too loud for conversation, allowing him a convenient excuse to retreat once more to silence. He was comfortable here, if a little cold.

A few days after his shopping trip with his mom, Casey called Matt and asked him to sell the guitar Casey had gotten two Christmases ago and send him the money.

"Why?" Matt asked.

"Because I don't like being broke." He leaned back on the sofa, feet dangling over the edge, phone cradled to his ear. "I hardly ever play the guitar anyway."

"Why don't you get a job?"

"I can't. I have to stay here and help Mom with Grandpa." He could hear some kind of machinery running in the background behind his brother. A wood chipper, or maybe a chain saw.

"How's he doing?"

"Okay. He can talk some now. He's not as grumpy, so I think maybe he feels better."

"How's Mom?"

"Okay. She looks tired. And kind of sad." He drew his knees up and wedged his toes beneath one bottom sofa cushion. "I don't know if it's because her dad is sick, or because she misses you and Dad and Denver."

"We miss her. Dad especially. The office is a mess without her."

"So what's it like, being a foreman?"

"Okay. Some of the older guys gave me a little grief, dissing me because I'm the boss's son, but I showed them I can work as hard as they do and I'm getting a little respect."

He hunched his shoulders against a stab of envy. He didn't think anyone had ever respected him, least of all his dad. "So is Dad pissed that I'm not there?"

"He was at first. He hasn't said anything lately. I guess it's good Mom's not down there by herself. He says he might try to take off a few days to come see y'all."

"That would be cool." He wasn't anxious to see his father if he was still upset with him, but Mom would probably appreciate a visit. "Hey, we got a dog."

"A dog? I thought Mom hated dogs."

"She doesn't hate dogs. She just never had one. She thought they were all dirty and everything, but this one's nice."

"What kind of dog?"

"I don't know. Part golden retriever, but something else, too. She has long gold hair and floppy ears and she smiles a lot."

"Dogs don't smile."

"This one does."

"What are you going to do when it's time to come home?"

"Bring her with us, you goof." It wasn't like they could leave Sadie here with Grandpa. Besides, Casey was her favorite person. The way he saw it, she was really his dog. "So will you sell the guitar?" he asked Matt.

"Why don't I just send you the money? You can pay me back later."

"You'd do that?"

"Yeah. I mean, you're a screw-up sometimes, but you're the only brother I got."

He swallowed around the lump in his throat. "Thanks."

"Yeah. You just remember you owe me."

"Right." When he got back home, maybe he'd quit charging Matt for using his hair gel. He'd even volunteer to clean Matt's side of the room for a week or so. That ought to be enough.

He didn't want to take this brotherly love thing too far.

CHAPTER 10

*I hope you love birds, too. It is economical. It saves
going to heaven.*
—*Emily Dickinson,* Life and Letters of Emily
Dickinson

"I stopped by to see if you and your father have managed to kill each other yet," Sara announced as she entered the kitchen one afternoon the first week in July.

"Why would you think we'd do that?" Karen asked.

"I spent a good part of the last years of my marriage wanting to strangle the man, and I have no doubt he felt the same about me." She deposited her purse on the counter and checked her hair in the reflection from the microwave door.

"You're exaggerating."

"Not by much." She sat at the table and looked around the room. "Never underestimate the ill will two people who were once in love can harbor against one another. Do you have any coffee?"

"I was just about to make a pot." She'd taken out the

coffee canister as soon as Sara walked into the house. Her mother lived on caffeine, martinis and deli salads, which perhaps explained why she still wore a size six at age sixty-nine.

"Where is my ex, anyway? I should say hello."

"He's working with the occupational therapist."

"He doesn't have an occupation, so what's the point? Though I suppose they could work on holding binoculars and typing on the computer."

"I believe they're doing something called 'fundamentals of daily living.' She's teaching Dad to dress himself, brush his teeth, maneuver his wheelchair, plus some speech therapy." It was depressing to think of a seventy-year-old man having to relearn how to tie his shoes, but the alternative was more horrible to contemplate.

"How's he doing with that?" Sara asked.

"All right, I guess. He gets frustrated and impatient, I think." Just last week, he'd thrown a shoe at the therapist, Lola.

"Martin can be a bear when he doesn't get his way, but then, can't we all?" She checked the coffeepot, then studied her manicure. "I saw your brother last night at Kelso's. He bought me a drink."

Kelso's was the local watering hole, a bar with pool tables upstairs and a big-screen TV in the main room, where matrons gathered for cocktails alongside beer-drinking truck drivers. Her brother and mother were both regulars. "What's Del up to?" Besides fishing, playing pool and avoiding responsibilities.

"The manager of his oil-change shop quit and the poor boy has been working himself near to death trying to keep things going." She took out an emery board and began filing her nails.

"I seriously doubt Del is in danger of working himself to death. Not as long as he has time to drink beer at Kelso's."

"Now, as a business owner yourself, you should know the kind of stress he's under. Nothing wrong with letting off a little steam." She put away the emery board. "Is that coffee ready yet?"

"I'll fix you a cup." She poured the coffee into an oversize mug, and added sugar and milk, reminded of mornings when she was a little girl when she'd beg for the privilege of fixing her parents' coffee. It had seemed such a grown-up thing to her then, and she always felt proud when they praised her for getting it "Just right."

She served the coffee and sat down across from her mother with her own cup. "I've taken up bird-watching," she said. "Dad is teaching me."

Sara made a face. "Please tell me you haven't inherited his crazy obsession with birds."

"No, but I'm enjoying it. It's very relaxing. Contemplative."

"That must be why I never cared for it. Of course, I

never liked yoga, either. I'd much rather *do* something than sit around meditating or whatever."

"Do you think if you'd shared Daddy's interest in birding, you'd have stayed together?"

Sara leveled a stern gaze at her daughter. "I never waste time contemplating what might have been. And your father and I had problems that went beyond common interests. The man is incapable of developing an emotional attachment to anyone."

The harshness of her words stung. "You make him sound like some kind of sociopath," Karen said. "Granted, he's reserved, but that doesn't mean he doesn't have feelings."

Sara's expression softened. "I hope you don't think taking up this hobby is going to give you some kind of instant spiritual connection to the man. Or that he'll suddenly grow all warm and sentimental."

"No, of course I don't think that." She shifted in her chair. If she couldn't have warm and sentimental, she'd settle for some sense of…closeness. Some sign that he was proud to have her as his daughter. That he loved her.

"You should get out of this house more. I've signed up for ice skating lessons at the rink over in Nacogdoches. You should join me."

"Ice skating? Mama, are you crazy? You could fall and break something."

"If I do, I know I can count on you to look after me."

Karen's heart stopped beating for a minute and she

sucked in her breath, a vision filling her head of her mother lying back in a hospital bed, issuing orders left and right.

"Don't look so horrified, dear." Sara laughed. "Oh my, I can see that would be your idea of hell—playing nursemaid to both of us at once." She sipped her coffee. "Well, don't worry. If I get sick I'm going to find some handsome male nurse to wait on me."

Except what were the odds of that happening? Her mother had no money, really. Not enough to pay for private care. There was no one else but Karen to come to her rescue. What she'd told herself would only be a few months' inconvenience could become years of being caught between the demands of her parents and her husband and children. The idea wrapped itself around her like a python, strangling her breath.

Lola emerged from Martin's bedroom, shutting the door softly behind her. "That's all for today," she said as she joined them in the kitchen.

"How did it go?" Karen asked.

"He didn't throw anything today, if that's what you mean." She grinned. She was a small, round woman with olive skin and almond-shaped eyes, her black hair cut very short all over and sticking out in all directions like quills on a porcupine.

"Would you like some coffee?" Karen asked, already reaching for a cup.

"That would be good." She set her bag of equipment on the floor. "Make it about half milk so I can drink it fast. I can't stay long."

"Have a seat." Sara nodded to the chair next to her. "I'm the ex-wife by the way. How's the old man doing?"

"He's making progress. Slowly. His speech is a little clearer, but there are things he needs to work on." She accepted the cup of coffee with a grateful look. "He's stubborn, which can be good and bad when it comes to therapy. It's good when they're determined to get well, bad when they resist going through the steps needed to get there."

"I can guess which kind of stubborn Martin is," Sara said. "He always hated being told what to do."

"I've dealt with worse." She smiled. "I can usually convince them to do things for their own good."

"So you think he's doing well?" Karen joined the women at the table. "I mean, well enough that he'll be able to talk again and do things for himself?"

"That's hard to say." Lola cradled the cup in both hands.

"What she really wants to know is, will he be able to live on his own again?" Sara said.

Lola shook her head. "At this stage, there's no way to know the answer to that. These things have to be taken in baby steps. Martin may never get back to the way he was, but the goal is to improve his quality of life and give him as much independence as possible."

Karen swallowed hard. "What will happen if he can't look after himself?"

"Then you may want to consider some sort of assisted living facility."

"A nursing home," Sara said.

"There are worse places to be," Lola said.

"I doubt my father would agree."

"The ideal situation would be for family to continue to look after him, but that isn't always possible." Lola drained her cup and set it on the table. "I'd better go now. I have one more client to see this afternoon."

"Thank you for everything." Karen walked her to the door. "I'll talk to Dad, see if I can't get him to be more cooperative."

"I'm sorry I couldn't give you a more definite prognosis, but I don't like to raise false hopes."

"I understand."

"Try not to worry." Lola patted her arm. "Whatever his final prognosis, you'll figure out what to do. Families always do."

Sure. She didn't bother telling Lola, but she'd ceased being the woman with all the answers six weeks ago somewhere between here and the Denver Airport.

Martin's body ached too much to let him sleep. Lola had been a tyrant today, demanding he bend and stretch and lift until he was in agony. She'd shown no pity, telling him over and over again that he had to challenge himself, to teach his dormant nerves and muscles to work properly again.

His spirit was bruised as well, from the shame of failing over and over at such simple tasks as buttoning his shirt correctly or cutting up food.

Lola had the grace not to comment on his fumbling, except to correct his mistakes and urge him to try harder.

It hadn't helped any that he'd gotten e-mails this morning from no less than three people in the birding community, crowing about their planned trips to Arkansas to look for the Ivory-billed Woodpecker—a species that until recently had been thought to be extinct. To add one to their personal list was now the holy grail of every birder. And Martin, though he lived only a few hours from the place where the woodpeckers had been found, was stuck, unable to move.

Sara had stopped by for a few minutes not long after Lola left. "How are you doing?" she'd asked, with real concern.

He'd shaken his head, and refused to say anything, his bad mood making conversation unwise. Though they'd been divorced for years, he still felt close enough to Sara to forgo politeness, and let her bear the brunt of his ill will, as he had too often in the latter days of their marriage.

"It's hell getting old," she'd said sympathetically. She patted his shoulder lightly, then sat across from him, on the side of the bed. "The therapist says you're doing pretty well for a stubborn old coot."

He'd always wondered how old men had come to be associated with a large black waterbird. As far as he knew, coots weren't particularly cantankerous.

"When this gets to be too tough, just remember it's not forever," Sara said. "I've found I can get through a lot of things that way."

He nodded. Had she gotten through their marriage that way? Maybe towards the end. In the early years they'd both believed in till death do us part. Only later did they realize how difficult, even impossible, that was sometimes.

"I won't wear you out chattering on. Just wanted to see how you're holding up." She stood, then bent to kiss his cheek. "Hang in there. You really are looking better."

He listened to her high heels clacking on the wood floor of the hallway as she left. Even at sixty-nine she still insisted on wearing heels and makeup and having her hair and nails done. "A high maintenance woman" one of his coworkers had labeled her, and it was true. But he'd never minded. Throughout his marriage, and even now, he hadn't lost his amazement that Sara Ellen Delwood had agreed to marry him.

When Martin was a teenager, he worked for a time for an old rancher, doing odd jobs and helping with the cattle. The old man had seen it as his duty to pass on advice to his young helper. On marriage, he'd been succinct: "Find the prettiest girl in town who will agree to sleep with you and stick with her," he'd said. "Unless you've got money or looks—and trust me, boy, you don't have neither—then you won't go wrong with that philosophy."

The first time he met Sara Delwood, Martin thought she was the prettiest girl he'd ever seen. He was too shy to ask her out, but she'd turned the tables and approached him first. "I was thinking about going into town and getting a hamburger and a malt," she'd said late one Friday after school. "Would you take me?"

He took her, and continued to escort her around all that summer and through their senior year. The night after graduation she'd turned to him and said. "Everybody thinks we've been dating so long we should get married. What do you think?"

So Sara had dragged him along with her into marriage and buying a house and having children and all the trappings of a conventional life. The only thing unconventional was his constant pursuit of birds. Eventually, the thing that had brought him the most peace and satisfaction in his life separated him from the family he'd acquired through no real effort of his own.

When she'd asked for the divorce, he hadn't argued. He had never completely lost the feeling that she deserved more than he could give her. He missed her for months—at times missed her still. But there was relief in being on his own, too, freedom from the guilt that he was letting someone else down when he focused on his passion for birds.

He was counting on that passion to get him through this rough time, as well. "You should set some goals for yourself," Lola had said. "It's good to give yourself something to aim for."

Goals. His goal was to get out of this bed and this house and back in the field. He wanted to go to Arkansas, and most especially, he wanted to return to Brazil. He had to find the Brown-chested Barbet. That one omission on his list loomed over his career like a dark cloud, overshadowing his other achievements. To be within a single species of cleaning up an entire country and not achieve that goal felt like the most ignoble failure.

How would he get there? He'd need help, obviously, though it pained him to admit it. A guide, then. Not one of those professional birding guides others hired to locate and point out the species for him. That wasn't true birding to him.

No, he needed someone to provide transportation to the area where the barbet would most likely be found. Someone to carry his bags and help him communicate with the natives.

Ed Delgado knew some people down there. Tomorrow Martin would e-mail and ask him for the names of some reliable guides. He wouldn't have the stamina he usually did; he'd have to allow for shorter days. He could go out early in the morning, then rest during the day and return at dusk, taking advantage of the prime hours for bird activity.

He'd have to be able to get around on his own more. He couldn't maneuver a wheelchair in the jungle. And he'd have to be able to talk to his interpreter. Lola had said with effort, and practice, he could do this thing. "Bar-bet." He tried the name on his tongue. To his ears, it sounded like *Ar-eth*.

"Bar-bet." He pressed his lips together to shape the *B*. Better that time. "Bor-ba." The name of the province he'd need to visit. "Ma-pi-a." The river where he'd be most likely to spot the barbet. The syllables were clumsy on his tongue. He repeated them over and over, mumbling to himself, trying to make the sounds as clear as he heard them in his head.

He fell asleep in a few moments, exhausted, birds darting through his dreams, elusive and always just beyond recognition.

Determined to force Del to do *something* to help her and his father, Karen knocked on his door one hot early July morning. As soon as he opened the door, she said, "The yard needs mowing. When can you do it?"

He looked over her shoulder at the overgrown yard and rubbed his chin. "It doesn't look that bad to me."

"Del, it's up past my ankles. And it looks terrible."

He shook his head. "Nobody around here really cares. The neighbors haven't complained."

"*I* care. I'm asking you to please mow it."

He sighed, the sound of a greatly burdened man. "All right, sis. I'll get around to it as soon as I can."

"That's not good enough, Del. I want you to do it today." Even as she listened to herself talk, part of her realized the unreasonableness of her request. Why should Del do anything she asked? Why should he try to please her now when he never had before?

But she couldn't stop herself from trying to berate him into behaving—just once—in the manner she thought he ought to behave. She wanted him to be the thoughtful, helpful brother she needed him to be right now. If he wouldn't do it voluntarily, then she would do her best to nag him into it.

"Can't. I've got plans."

"Then change them."

He stood back a little and looked her up and down. "Your problem, sis, is that you're too uptight. You need to learn to relax and go with the flow."

"Uh-huh. And while I'm relaxing, who's going to do all the work that needs doing around here?" How many times had she said that before—begging the boys to clean their rooms or nagging Tom into catching up on his share of the paperwork at the office.

"Maybe some of it won't get done." He shrugged. "It won't be the end of the world." He stood up straighter.

"I've got an idea. Why don't I take you out Saturday night? Casey can look after Dad for a few hours. Take your mind off your worries for a while."

A night out with Del? "Where would you take me?"

"Oh, you know. Just around."

She shook her head. "I don't think so."

"Why not? Are you afraid you might have a good time for a change?"

She flinched at this dig. "No, that's not it. I just don't think your idea of fun and mine are the same."

"You know what they say—when in Rome... I think you're scared you might find out the two of us aren't so different after all—that you're not as smart and sophisticated as you like to pretend, and that I'm not the dumb hick you make me out to be."

Ouch! He made her sound so snobby. "I've never thought you were dumb." Lazy, immoral, dishonest and sneaky, but never dumb.

"Then I dare you to go out with me. Just once. Don't be afraid to have a good time." He winked. "You might even find out I'm not so bad after all."

His smile made her remember the Del who had been her childhood playmate, the one who had always been able to make her laugh—the one she still loved. Maybe this was his way of extending an olive branch, offering them the chance to be friends again. "If I go out with you, will you mow the lawn?"

"You bet. First free day I get."

It wasn't the answer she wanted, but she sensed it was the best she was going to get. "All right," she said. "I'll go out with you." Who knows, she might enjoy herself. Or even learn to enjoy her brother again.

CHAPTER 11

You cannot fly like an eagle with the wings of a wren.
—*William Henry Hudson*, Afoot in England

The interior of Del's truck reminded Karen of a frat house she'd visited once, with the same crushed beer cans and pizza boxes on the floorboards, the same odor of stale pot clinging to the upholstery and—she could have sworn—the same black silk thong hanging from the rearview mirror.

She stepped gingerly over the trash and settled into the seat. "Don't you ever clean this thing?"

"I was in a hurry." He leaned across her and swept all the garbage out into the yard.

"Del, you can't just leave all that trash lying there."

"I'll get it when we get home."

She frowned, knowing he'd never remember. Which meant she'd be out there in the morning, cursing him for being a slob.

She took a deep breath and leaned back in the seat. She'd promised herself she wasn't going to get into a fight with her brother tonight. She was going to take his advice, relax and have a good time.

"Where are we going?" she asked as she pulled on the too-tight safety belt that had her pinned in her seat.

"Somewhere you wouldn't be caught dead in by yourself, that's for sure." The headlights of oncoming cars illuminated his face. He was grinning, the look of the bratty little brother who'd just put a frog in his sister's bed.

Actually, it had been a lizard, which had remained hidden until ten-year-old Karen switched off the light and crawled into bed. Five minutes later she stood in the middle of the bedroom, screaming at the top of her lungs while the lizard clung to her long brown hair like a kid on a wild carnival ride. Del stood outside her door, bent double with laughter, while her father bellowed at them to all be quiet and her mother chided Karen for being hysterical.

She liked to think she'd grown out of that kind of hysteria. If this evening proved to be the adult version of the lizard-in-the-bed, she'd get through it without losing her cool. And when she got back to the house, she'd start plotting her revenge.

"How's the dog?" Del asked.

"The dog is fine." Somehow, Sadie had found a soft spot in Karen's heart. Whether it was the dog's liquid brown eyes, or her habit of resting in the evenings with her head against Karen's feet as Karen watched television, or Sadie's obvious adoration of Casey, Karen no longer thought of her as a dirty beast to be tolerated, but as another part of the household, like Mary Elisabeth or Lola.

"I knew she'd grow on you. Dogs have a way of doing that."

"Then why don't you have one?" she asked.

"I did. A chihuahua named Max." He laughed. "Can you believe that—me with a little nothing of a dog like that?"

"What happened to him?" she asked, almost afraid to hear the answer.

"Sheila took him with her when she split. Said she didn't trust me to look after him."

Karen made a snorting sound. She'd always known Sheila had good sense.

Del switched on the radio and the plaintive voice of a country singer moaned about his sorry lot in life. Karen looked out the side window of the pickup, at the seedy taverns and ramshackle houses that dotted the roadside, each one illuminated in the rosy glow of a mercury vapor light, like tawdry jewels on display. "I never should have let you talk me into this," she said.

"But you did. Couldn't hardly believe it myself. Now relax. If you let yourself you might even have fun tonight."

"I don't want to have fun."

He chuckled. "There's your problem in a nutshell."

He, on the other hand, never wanted anything but fun.

He turned off the road into a gravel parking lot. Karen stared at the sprawling, squat-roofed building before them. The Bait Shop, proclaimed the red neon sign over the door.

"I would have thought this place would have burned down by now," she said as Del shut off the engine.

"Nah, it'll be here when your grandkids are looking for a place to party."

She followed him across the gravel lot. Local lore held that the original owner of the bar had named it so that local husbands could go out drinking while truthfully telling their wives they were headed to the bait shop.

Gleaming Harleys and dented pickup trucks crowded the small parking area. Inside, most of the light was provided by a dozen or more neon beer signs. Cigarette smoke fogged the air, and the clack of pool balls provided a staccato counterpart to Aerosmith on the jukebox.

"Don't wrinkle your nose that way," Del said. "It's unattractive." He grabbed her elbow and pulled her toward the back of the bar. "Come on, let's play some pool."

They found an empty table. Del fed in three quarters and began racking up the balls while Karen selected a cue.

"Hey, Del, who's your new honey?" A short man

with the most freckles Karen had ever seen came up to them.

"Lay off, Eddie. This is my sister, Karen."

Eddie sobered and tugged on the brim of his gimme cap. "Nice to meet you, Miss Karen." He grinned. "Never would have thought an ugly old cuss like Del would have such a pretty sister."

She flushed in spite of herself. Of course Eddie was spouting hot air, but it had been a long time since a man had told her she was pretty.

"Pay attention, sis. It's your shot."

She bent over the table, trying to remember everything she'd learned as a teen, in the hours spent wielding a pool cue in the back room of the convenience store/bar a few blocks from the house. She aimed carefully, and missed.

"Out of practice, are you?" Del moved to make his next shot.

Eddie was still standing there, staring at her in a way she found unnerving. "How do you know my brother?" she asked.

"Eddie works for me at the oil-change shop," Del said, moving around to make another shot.

Eddie nodded. "Been there a year now. Best job I ever had."

It dawned on Karen that Eddie was what they used to refer to as *slow*. Not the brightest bulb in the chandelier. "That's nice. So Del's a good boss to work for?"

Eddie's grin broadened. "The best. A few months

back, my trailer was broke into and the thieves made off with my television and stereo and everything. Wouldn't have been so bad, but my wife was seven months pregnant and the doctor had put her on bed rest. Watching TV was the only entertainment she had. Next thing I know, Del's over there hooking up a fancy thirty-inch color television. Said it was an extra one he had around the house and he wanted us to have it."

Karen glanced at her brother, who was at the opposite end of the table, frowning at a difficult shot. "Del did that?"

"Yeah. And come to find out, it wasn't no spare set at all. It was his own television." Eddie's voice wavered and he looked at the floor and cleared his throat. "I never had nobody do nothing like that for me before."

"Don't pay attention to him, sis. He exaggerates." Del clapped Eddie on the shoulder. "Why don't you go ask the waitress to bring us some beer?"

When Eddie had left them, Karen turned to Del. "Did you really do that? Did you give him your TV?"

He shrugged. "It's not like I'm home much to watch it, anyway. And I did have a little set in the bedroom until Sheila split and took it with her." He nudged her arm. "Now go on, make your next shot."

She managed to sink two balls in a row before missing one. Eddie returned with three beers and handed one to each of them. "Thanks," she said.

Two more men, Troy and Frank, joined them.

They'd been friends with Del since high school, and it surprised her a little to see the gawky teens she remembered grown up into muscular men. "Nice to see you, Karen," Frank said, nodding to her. "Del says you've been working hard, looking after your dad."

She still found it hard to believe Del had been saying nice things about her to his friends. She certainly never went out of her way to speak highly of him.

More people came in, all hailing Del, clapping him on the back, offering to buy him a beer. Karen would have said he was the most popular man in the place. But why? What was it about him that made people like him so? And what did it say about her that she couldn't see it?

She had her back to the main bar, focusing on making her next shot, when a woman's voice cut through the jumble of conversation around her. "Delwood Engel, does that floozy you've been sleeping with know you've got a new one on the side?"

Karen straightened and turned to see Sheila, the former Mrs. Delwood Engel, headed toward them, fire in her eyes. The crowd around them pulled back like a receding tide, leaving Del and Karen alone under the pool table light.

"You need to have your eyes checked, Sheila," Del drawled. He picked up a square of chalk and began chalking his pool cue. "Don't tell me you've forgotten my sister, Karen."

Sheila stopped short, and stared at Karen. Then a

smile broke across her face and she held her arms wide. "Karen! Hon, it's so good to see you." She surrounded Karen in a crushing hug, then drew back to look at her again. "I knew you were in town but I never dreamed I'd find you here with that skunk of a brother of yours."

"Del talked me into taking a night off," she said weakly. "Casey's watching Dad."

"How's that little boy of yours doing?" Sheila asked. "Although I guess he's not that little anymore, is he?"

"He's sixteen and six feet tall," Karen said.

"I wish I could see him. Tell him his Aunt Sheila said hello." She kept one arm around Karen and turned her away from the pool table. "Let's find a spot to sit and visit a little."

Karen always had liked Sheila. And the chance to hear her side of her split with Del was too tempting to pass up. She turned and handed her pool cue to Eddie. "Take over for me, will you?" she said. "I'm not very good at this anyway."

Sheila led her to an empty booth within sight of the pool tables, but far enough away they wouldn't be heard. "So tell me what you've been up to," she said. "How's your dad? And Tom and the boys?"

"They're all good. Well, Dad's been better, but he's recovering. Making progress every day."

"You know if there's anything at all I can do, I will. I felt terrible about not getting over there to the house as soon as I heard, but my lawyer told me until the divorce is final, it'd be best to keep my distance."

"So it's not final yet?" Karen asked.

"We finally have the court date, in a couple of weeks." She fished in her purse and took out a pack of cigarettes. "Mind if I smoke?"

Karen shook her head. Sheila shook out a cigarette and lit it from a red lighter that matched the red of her long nails. She had bleached blond hair piled high on her head, and a long face, deep furrows on either side of her mouth. Not the beauty Mary Elisabeth was, but she'd stood by Del longer than any of his other wives or girlfriends. Karen had to think there'd been some real feeling between them at one time. "If you don't think I'm being too nosy, what was the delay?" she asked.

"Del owed his lawyer money, so the lawyer wouldn't file the right papers until he got paid." Sheila waved cigarette smoke away from them. "But I guess he found the money somewhere and finally paid the bill, so things are good to go."

So Del had been telling the truth about why he needed the money from their dad. "I was sorry to hear about y'all splitting up," Karen said. "But I can't say I blame you."

"Best decision I ever made," Sheila said. "I don't know why I didn't do it sooner."

"It's not easy to decide to end a marriage," Karen said. "Especially when you love someone."

"Yeah, but after a while it wasn't so much love as habit." She took another long pull on the cigarette, the end glowing red. "It's easier to stay with what you know—even if you're miserable—than it is to cut loose and face the scary things you don't know." She shrugged. "I don't think I realized how miserable I was until I left him and started living on my own."

"I'm glad you're doing well."

"Honey, I'm doing great!" Sheila's grin lit up her face. "I married my first husband when I was seventeen, and pretty much went straight from his house to Del's. I'm living on my own for the first time in my life. I can cook what I want for dinner, when I want to, watch what I want on TV, have a whole bathroom to myself without tripping over his dirty clothes or wet towels." She stabbed out the stub of the cigarette in a glass ashtray. "Except for the having kids thing, which I never did, I don't know why any woman would bother with getting married these days. There's just so much more freedom in being single, you know?"

Karen nodded, though she didn't know. Not really. She'd gone from her parents' house to Tom's and never thought much about it. What would it be like to have only herself to answer to? Lonely. Then again, she might find out she was pretty good company for herself.

"Gawd, here I am going on and on about myself. What have you been up to?"

"Taking care of Dad and Casey." And before that,

she'd been taking care of Tom and the two boys, and looking after their business. She didn't even have any interesting hobbies to talk about.

"You still in the landscaping business up there in Denver?"

She nodded. "It's doing really well. Matt is working for us now, too."

Or rather, he was working for Tom. The business was really Tom's. Karen had the title of office manager, but she deferred to Tom on all but the simplest business decisions. "Are you still working for the school district?" she asked.

Sheila nodded. "I'll have been there twenty years in September. But I'm also doing sales on the side."

She dug in her purse and pulled out a business card. The mauve lettering on a pale pink background announced that Sheila Engel was a Mary Kay representative.

"You need anything while you're in town, give me a call. Or maybe you can come over one day and let me give you a free facial. We have some great products I know you'd love."

Karen nodded weakly. "Thanks."

Sheila checked her watch and jumped up. "I've got to go or I'm gonna be late." She winked at Karen. "I've got a date. Real nice guy." She laid a five on the table and weighed it down with the ashtray. "When the waitress comes by, tell her that's for my drink." She leaned down and hugged Karen, smothering her in the scent of Shalimar and cigarette smoke. "I'll call you sometime, okay. You take care."

She hurried away, leaving Karen to ponder how much she had in common with her soon-to-be-former sister-in-law, and how differently their lives had turned out.

She was still sitting there when Del found her. "Sheila get tired of bad-mouthing me and leave?" he asked.

"She said she had a date."

"Hmph. I ought to find out who it is and send the guy a sympathy card." He looked around the bar. The crowd had thinned and the jukebox had switched to mournful Hank Williams. "This place is dead. Let's go find some action somewhere else."

Karen followed him out to his truck. "I think I want to go home," she said.

"Home? The night is young." He unlocked her door, then went around the driver's side.

"I know, but I'm tired. And I don't like leaving Dad at night like this."

"Casey's with him. He'll be okay." He started the truck and backed out of his parking space.

"Casey's still only sixteen." And not the most mature sixteen-year-old she'd ever met. "What if Dad falls?" Her stomach clenched at the thought. "Or what if he chokes? He still has trouble swallowing sometimes and—"

"What if he does?" Del's voice was cold. He turned

onto the highway and sped up. "It wouldn't be the end of the world."

She caught her breath and stared at him. "Del! You don't mean that. He's your father."

He glanced at her, his expression as calm as if they were discussing whether or not the fish were biting. "How much difference is it really going to make to you if he's dead or alive?"

"It will make a difference." Surely it would.

"Not to me it won't. And if he dies, at least I stand to inherit a little dough."

"Del, you don't mean that."

He glanced at her again. "You think I'm the world's biggest bastard for using the old man for whatever I can get, but I don't believe you're any better."

"What do you mean? I've never asked him for a dime. And I put aside everything to come down here to look after him."

"Yeah, but why would you do that? It's not as if you were close to him before. It's not like he'd do the same for you."

"You don't know that—"

"Hear me out." He held up one hand. "You see, I'm thinking you rushed down here because you want something from the old man. It's not about him at all. It's about what you think he's going to give you."

"That's not true!" *Was it?* "Wanting to have a relationship with my father isn't a bad thing," she protested.

"What about what he wants? He was okay with keeping his distance for forty years. Why should he change now?"

"I can't believe he wants to spend the rest of his life alone."

"Some people do. And some of them are perfectly happy doing it. Or as happy as they ever get."

He made a sharp turn onto a side road, throwing her against the passenger door. "Del, slow down!"

He ignored her, and punched the accelerator harder. "So see, I'm not the only selfish one in this family. Just because you want something more *noble* than money doesn't mean you aren't using him the same way I am."

She braced herself with one hand on the dash. Why hadn't she had the sense to call a cab from the bar? Del was in no condition to drive. And he had no business second-guessing her motives for being here.

"All right, what if Dad thinks he's content being so distant from his children? That doesn't mean he's right."

Del eased off the gas and slowed the truck. "Haven't you heard the expression, you can't teach an old dog new tricks?"

"We're not talking about learning to sit or roll over. We're talking about communicating. Getting to know each other. We've got time now to try. Time we never really had before."

He shook his head. "You talk like those things aren't a lot harder than sitting up and rolling over." His face had gone slack and he looked tired, and much older. And more like Martin than Karen would have thought possible. "You'd be better off making your peace with the old man, the way I have."

"You mean giving up."

"I'm not beating my head against the wall and trying to change somebody who won't change, if that's what you mean."

"People can change." She'd changed, just in the few weeks she'd been here. She'd started to look at her life and herself differently. To see possibilities she'd never considered before. All these new choices were both scary and exciting.

"Go ahead then," Del said as he turned onto the road leading to her father's house. "It's your funeral. But stop lying to yourself and pretending you're only here for him."

She closed her eyes and leaned her head back. "All right, I've heard you. You can shut up now." She didn't want to listen to him anymore. What if she was here because she wanted something from her father, and not purely out of daughterly devotion? Was that so bad? Considering how many years she'd spent helping her husband, raising children and running a household and a business, maybe it was time she did something that was purely selfish.

Two days later, having given up on Del, Karen asked Casey to mow the lawn for her. He promised he would, then left to go fishing, taking Sadie with him. So Karen found herself one hot afternoon the next week in the shed behind the house, pouring gas into the tank of the riding lawn mower and cursing the men in her life.

Del should have done this. She wasn't buying any of his excuses. She tossed the empty gas can aside and replaced the tank lid, wrinkling her nose at the sour smell of the gas. This was one more example of the way he slacked off on his responsibilities. Would it have killed him to help her with this one thing?

Her feelings toward Casey were more mixed. She was annoyed with him for not fulfilling his promise before taking off to go fishing. At the same time, she was reluctant to come down too hard on him. How many boys his age would want to spend the summer helping to look after his grandfather and doing chores? He deserved some down time.

Tom would say she was being too soft on him, that a boy should keep his commitments. And he was right. But Casey was her baby, and he wouldn't be hers much longer. She didn't want to be the bad guy all the time with him. Not when he responded to kindness with smiles and hugs—something she didn't get nearly enough of these days.

She turned the key and breathed a sigh of relief as the motor turned over. Carefully, she backed the mower out of the shed and started toward the house. As she passed the front porch, she waved to her father, who didn't wave back. Maybe he'd fallen asleep. She'd parked his wheelchair in the deepest shade of the porch, and made sure his binoculars and a bottle of ice water with a straw were within easy reach. He was getting better at maneuvering with one hand, though his left side was still mostly useless. At the suggestion of the nurse's aide, she'd hung a whistle around his neck that he could blow if he needed her. She wasn't sure if she could hear it over the roar of the mower, but she figured it was worth a try.

The sun beat down like a hundred-watt bulb in an interrogation room. She could feel it burning the top of her head even through her hat. Within five minutes, sweat soaked through her shirt and ran in rivulets to pool between her breasts. Conditioned by years of warnings to avoid the sun in Denver's thin atmosphere, she'd dressed for this job in jeans and a long-sleeved denim shirt, broad-brimmed hat and hiking boots. She didn't have to worry about sunburn, but heat stroke might very well do her in.

When she was a teenager, she'd mowed the lawn wearing a bikini top, cutoff shorts and grass-stained Keds. The object was to work on her tan while doing her chores. It didn't hurt her feelings any when the local boys drove by and honked their horns and whistled as she buzzed the mower along the front fence line.

Come to think of it, the most vocal argument she

and her father had ever had happened when she was sixteen and she'd headed for the lake wearing a minuscule crocheted bikini and a see-through gauze coverup. He'd ordered her to return to the house and put on *real clothes*. His face had turned an alarming shade of red and he'd literally sputtered when he talked. At the time, Karen had dismissed him as a clueless old man out to ruin her life. She smiled, remembering. As a parent herself now, she understood his concern. And it touched her to remember how much he'd cared, even if only about her appearance.

The heat and the steady roar of the mower lulled her into a stupor. Each pass across the yard showed a broader expanse of neatly cropped grass. If only everything in her life was so easily put in order. Maybe that was the real appeal of the landscaping business to Tom. The results of hard work were almost immediately visible and satisfying.

She finished the front yard in less than an hour and drove the mower around back. There was twice as much area to cover here, including the sloping banks around the pond. She shut the mower off and stared at the expanse of overgrown grass, tips burned brown by the sun. The pond sat like a mirage at the far end of the lot, its muddy surface smooth as a piece of slate.

She climbed off the mower and went inside to check on her father and get a drink of water before tackling the rest of the work. Dad was dozing in his chair, shoulders slumped, chin resting on his chest. The electric fan she'd set up near the steps stirred a few strands of his gray hair, and she curled her fingers against her palm to keep from reaching out and brushing it back from his forehead, afraid she might wake him. Instead, she indulged in the luxury of studying him while he was unaware of her presence.

The stroke had aged him, etching new lines on his forehead, deepening the furrows alongside his mouth, which still drooped slightly on the left side. The skin beneath his jaw sagged into jowls, freckled with age spots, testament to the years he'd spent in the sun. His nose was straight and prominent as ever, and his high, domed forehead made her think of the busts of elder statesmen that ringed the rotunda of the state capital in Austin.

She'd have to see about cutting his hair later today. And maybe a shave, too. She didn't like to see him looking like some unkempt old man. Though unconcerned about keeping up with fashion, he'd always been meticulous about his appearance, and even in the jungle wore pressed khakis and starched shirts.

Funny, that she knew so much about him, even after so many years of scarcely talking. It was as if some part of her had filed away every scrap of information about him, until she'd assembled enough to form this image she'd labeled Father.

Did he know as much about her? Were her characteristics and habits as important to him as those of the hundreds of birds he'd cataloged?

She turned the fan to blow less directly on him, and added ice to his water bottle, then went to complete her mowing.

She was making her first pass by the pond when something exploded up out of the grass, startling her. She squealed and rose half out of her seat, killing the mower engine. A bird flew by her, so near she could hear the rub of feather on feather as it turned to make another pass by her. She had an image of a brownish back and white chest with two black bands. A Killdeer.

As she watched, the bird plummeted to the ground and began dragging itself across the grass, one wing trailing behind it. Horrified, Karen thought it must have somehow been hit by the mower.

Then something she'd read in the field guide her father had given her made her relax a little. Killdeer would feign a broken wing in order to lead predators away from their nest.

A nest! She eased off the mower and took a cautious step forward. There, behind a clump of weeds, she spotted the shallow, dish-shaped nest. The mother bird tilted her head and studied her with one red-ringed eye. Karen was amazed the bird hadn't abandoned the nest with the mower bearing down on her, but instead had left it to her mate to defend her.

But then, that was the essence of mother love,

wasn't it—that desperate feeling that you would do anything to keep your young from harm, even exposing yourself to danger for their sake.

Shaken by the thought, she returned to the mower and shoved the gearshift into reverse. Straining, she pushed the heavy machine away from the nest, waiting until she was some distance away before switching it back on. The rest of the mowing could wait, until she'd made sure there were no other mothers and their young in harm's way.

Back at the house, she found her father awake. "You...through?" he asked, shifting in his chair.

"Not exactly." She looked toward the backyard, then at him again. "Can I take you to see something? Something I found near the pond?"

He frowned at her, then nodded. "Okay." Conversation was limited to one and two word answers these days, but it was a step above typing everything on the computer.

It took some maneuvering to get him down the ramp out front (which Del had finally replaced, after much nagging from her and Mary Elisabeth) and around to the backyard. The wheelchair didn't roll well over the rough ground and by the time they neared the nest Karen was sweating and panting. She drew as close as she dared, then set the chair's brake. "It's a nest. In the grass there. Do you see?" She pointed.

He leaned forward a little, squinting. "Kill...deer." He shaped the words carefully, halting but clear.

"I almost ran over it with the mower. The male flew up in my face at the last minute. The female sat there, never even moving."

"Birds…are…good parents. Most of 'em." He looked at her, his gaze intent. "Better…than some…people."

It was the longest sentence he'd uttered in months, and the effort visibly drained him. He sagged in his chair, slumped to one side. She hurried to prop him up, her arms around him, hugging tightly as she swallowed tears. Was he talking about the job he'd done as parent to her? Or her efforts to raise Casey and Matt? Whether confession or acknowledgment, his words touched her. "People do the best they can," she murmured, her lips against the top of his head, where the pink scalp showed through the thin hair. "We all do the best we can."

CHAPTER 12

Hope is the thing with feathers
That perches in the soul,
And sings the tune without the words,
And never stops at all.
—Emily Dickinson, "No. 254"

The summer monsoons descended on Denver in mid-July and Tom decided he could afford to take a long weekend away from the business to visit Texas. Karen met him at the Houston airport on a scorching Saturday morning. They embraced at the baggage claim, holding each other tightly for a long moment, until he finally broke apart and looked down at her. "How in the hell do you stand this heat?" he asked.

She laughed, and he joined in. "That's a fine way to say hello," she said.

"I'm sorry. You look great. I've missed you. How's that?"

"Better. I've missed you, too." She'd forgotten how tall and broad-shouldered and absolutely *masculine* he was. Standing here next to him, her body was reminding her of all the wonderful things he could make her feel, and that it had been seven weeks, six days and twenty-two hours since they'd last made love. If it weren't for the fact that they'd suffocate in this heat, she'd have been tempted to drive to some deserted forest road and start ripping his clothes off.

They collected his suitcase and walked to the parking garage. "Where's Casey?" he asked.

"He's back at the house with Dad." She looked up at him, searching his face. "He thinks you're still mad at him."

"I'm not exactly thrilled with him, but I'm pretty much over being angry." He glanced at her. "Wouldn't do any good, anyway, would it?"

"Let him know you're glad to see him. It would mean a lot to him."

"What do you think I'm going to do—yell at him the minute I see him?"

"No. Yes." She shook her head. "I don't know. I can never be sure how the two of you are going to act around each other."

"You worry too much. It'll be all right." He stowed his suitcase in the back and took the keys from her hand. "How's your dad?"

"Good. He's talking in sentences more now. He's eating better and he's starting to put on weight. I'm really encouraged."

"That's good." He started the Jeep, then leaned over

and studied the dashboard. "How do you turn the air conditioner up in this thing?"

On the drive to the house, Tom filled her in on his progress with various jobs at work, and happenings around the house. Her roses were blooming. Matthew had collected all the paperwork he needed to register for the fall semester at Red Rocks. He and Audra were definitely dating again. The car needed the front end aligned. The temporary worker was making progress with the paperwork at the office.

Karen sat back and listened, absorbing these petty details of her normal life like a dry tree soaking its roots in a flood. This was what she'd missed most, without even realizing it, this feeling of being a part of the minutiae of her husband's and son's lives. Not knowing the little things that affected them had made her feel too much of an outsider.

At the house, Tom parked the car in the shade and followed her inside. Casey met them at the front door, and took Tom's suitcase without being asked. "Hey, Dad," he said. "How was your trip?"

"It was fine." Tom put his arm around Casey's shoulder and pulled him close. "How are you doing? You look like you've grown another two inches since I saw you last."

Casey grinned. "Three."

Karen felt more of the tension ease from her body. All the pieces of her life were slipping back into their familiar grooves once more.

"Who's this?" Tom asked, directing his attention to Sadie, who inserted her body between Casey and his father, her whole body vibrating.

"This is Sadie." Casey patted the dog's head. "Uncle Del gave her to us."

Tom's eyes met Karen's over the top of Casey's bent head. "I thought you didn't like dogs."

She flushed. "I didn't. I still don't. But Sadie…Sadie's okay."

"She's a great dog," Casey said. "And really smart. I taught her to sit and stay and she hasn't messed in the house once."

If you didn't count hair, muddy paw prints and the occasional flea, Karen thought. Still, the dog had turned out better than she'd anticipated.

The creak of her father's wheelchair on the hardwood floor announced his arrival. He emerged from the hallway and looked up at his son-in-law. "Tom!"

Tom moved forward to take Martin's hand. "It's good to see you. I was sorry to hear about your stroke, but Karen tells me you're doing well with your rehabilitation."

"Too…slow," her father said.

Sara arrived soon after that, then Del and Mary Elisabeth, everyone flocking to greet the newcomer. Sometimes Karen thought her family liked Tom better than they did her. Then again, it was probably easier to like someone with whom you didn't share so much history.

The rest of the afternoon disappeared in a rush to

prepare food for everyone. She and Mary Elisabeth chopped vegetables, marinated chicken, passed out paper plates and fixed glass after glass of iced tea. Normally she enjoyed playing hostess, but today all she really wanted to do was get Tom alone. They exchanged glances over the heads of the others and she could have sworn she saw the same longing in his eyes.

"While you're here, I should take you fishing," Del said in between bites of potato salad. "I know some great spots."

"Maybe some other time." Tom smiled at Karen. "I'm only going to be here a few days. I want to spend them with Karen and Casey."

"Isn't that sweet?" Sara beamed at them over the rim of her coffee cup. "Karen Anne, what did you ever do to land a man like that?"

"Just lucky, I guess." What but luck could explain how two people who had hardly known each other when they said vows had stayed together all these years?

Luck, or the power of inertia, a voice whispered in her head.

Finally, the last of the potato salad was eaten, the last piece of chicken consigned to the refrigerator, the last of the tea poured from the pitcher. "All right, everyone." Sara stood and gathered up her purse. "Time for us to leave these two alone. I'm sure they've had enough of us all interfering with their reunion."

Karen flushed, but gave her mom a grateful smile.

"Don't do anything I wouldn't do," Del said as he and Mary Elisabeth headed for the door.

"Of course, there isn't much he wouldn't do," Mary Elisabeth added with a wink.

"I'll help Granddad get ready for bed," Casey said, taking hold of Martin's chair.

When they were alone at last, Karen felt as awkward as a girl on her first date. She busied herself tidying up the already clean kitchen. "Everyone was really glad to see you," she said.

"Not half as glad as I am to see you." He took a glass from her hand and set it aside, then turned her to face him. "Come here. We have some catching up to do."

His kiss was urgent, telling her in more than words how much he'd missed her. She clung to him, sinking into the luxury of that kiss, yet wanting so much more.

Scarcely moving apart, they fumbled their way to her bedroom and shut the door behind them. He led her to the bed, already removing his shirt as he moved. She lay back, watching him, grinning. Working outdoors had kept him lean and hard, the kind of man who made any woman look twice. More than once she'd visited a job site and found women admiring him, and had the satisfaction of informing them that he was her husband. "Are you going to do a striptease for me?"

"I don't know. Maybe we should get you out of your clothes first." He knelt on the bed beside her and reached for the top button of her blouse.

She stifled laughter, and glanced nervously toward the wall behind her, that separated her bedroom from Casey's. "We have to be quiet," she whispered.

"I can be quiet. Can you?" He nuzzled her neck, setting her to giggling again.

She tried to relax as he began working on her blouse once more, but it was impossible now that she'd reminded herself they weren't alone in the house.

Tom noticed her tension. "What's wrong?" he asked.

"I can't relax with my dad and Casey just a few rooms over." She sat up and tugged the quilt from around the pillows. "Come on. I've got an idea."

Quilt in hand, she led him out of the room and across the kitchen floor, tiptoeing. Once they were out the back door, she grabbed his hand and started across the yard.

The air was only slightly cooler than it had been that morning, but not as heavy. Dusk bathed everything in silver light and the first stars were already showing against the pale sky. They walked the path around the pond, to the back of the storage shed. "No one can see us here," she said, spreading the quilt on the ground.

He knelt and pulled her down beside him. "We haven't made love outside in a long time," he said.

"We haven't made love at all in a long time." She took hold of the unbuttoned halves of his shirt and pushed them back over his shoulders, and kissed the bare skin along his collarbone. He smelled of herbal soap and clean sweat and tasted slightly salty.

He finished undoing her blouse, then helped her out of her pants, stripping off his own clothes soon after. They came together with heat and urgency, done with waiting. They moved with a confidence born of familiarity, yet with a sense of discovering each other all over again. She delighted in knowing she could still move him, that he remembered where to touch her to make her pant with need, that he could still bring her to shuddering climax.

When they were spent, they lay together, wrapped in the quilt, looking up at the stars, a dreamlike quality to the moment. A Chuck-will's-widow sounded its mournful call: chuck-will's-WID-ow! Chuck-will's-WID-ow!

"Dad's been teaching me about birds some," she said, her head resting on his chest. The steady beat of his heart echoed in her ear and she found herself matching her breathing to his.

"I didn't think you were interested in that kind of thing."

"I wasn't. But it gives us something to talk about. And it is fascinating, in a way. All the different birds and their habits. Plus, they're beautiful to watch."

"Yeah. I guess so." His voice was slurred, that of a man fighting sleep and losing the battle. She snuggled closer and his arms automatically tightened around her. It felt so good to be here with him again. She'd known that seeing each other face to face would dissolve the barriers communicating only by phone had thrown up between them. Now that Tom was here, now that he could see Dad's condition and how much she was needed, he'd understand why she had no choice but to be here for this little while. Soon, everything would be all right again. She'd be home, the business would be running smoothly, the boys would be settled. Everything would be as it should be and it would be almost as if this summer had never happened.

The idea brought a surge of relief. Maybe all the unsettled feelings she had since coming here were merely a product of being away from her familiar routine. Maybe the only thing she really needed to change was her location. Back among the familiar, everything would fall into place again.

It was a comforting thought, and she drifted off to sleep cradled in Tom's arms, relieved to know this was exactly where she needed to be.

Karen woke Sunday morning with the comforting weight of Tom in bed beside her. She rolled over to face him, smiling, and he opened one eye and looked at her. "So I didn't dream this last night," he said.

"No, you didn't dream it."

He pulled her close and nuzzled her neck. "And that really was you screaming my name under the stars."

She giggled as he nipped her earlobe. "That really was me."

"I think I'm ready for a repeat." He moved closer, leaving no doubt about how ready he was.

She looked at the clock. It was after eight. "I don't know if I have time. I don't usually sleep this late—"

"Sure you have time." He nudged her legs apart with his knee and slipped his hand beneath the oversize T-shirt that served as her nightgown.

"Dad needs help getting ready in the morning," she protested.

"It won't hurt him to wait." He tugged the T-shirt up to her neck. "I came a thousand miles to see you. You can make a little time for me."

"Of course I can." She took a deep breath and focused her attention on him. He was right. A few minutes wouldn't make any difference.

She pulled off the T-shirt and helped him out of his boxers, then closed her eyes and lost herself in the sensation of his mouth on her throat, her breasts, her stomach....

The bell began ringing just as Tom settled between her legs. "What the hell is that?" he asked.

"Dad. He rings the bell when he wants me."

She started to sit, but Tom pushed her back. "He can wait."

"What if he's fallen or something?"

"He hasn't fallen. He'll be okay. Besides, Casey will answer him in a minute."

"You know how Casey is. He could sleep through a train wreck."

Tom nudged her thighs farther apart. "Pretend you're a teenager again, getting away with something right under Daddy's nose. And I'm the bad boy next door."

His grin was wickedly sexy, and she managed a weak laugh. She wanted to play along with his fantasy, to forget about worries and responsibilities in his arms, but the insistent ringing of the little brass handbell bored into her brain.

She lay back on the pillows and squeezed her eyes shut, straining to focus on Tom, but the moment was lost. She felt stiff and uncomfortable, impatient for him to be done.

She went through the motions of making love, saying the right things and making the right moves, but she'd never thought of herself as an accomplished actress, and she was afraid Tom knew her heart wasn't in the moment.

When he'd withdrawn from her, she sat up and threw back the covers. The bell continued to ring. "I guess I'd better go see what he wants," she said with a smile of apology.

Tom frowned and turned away.

Her father was upset at having to wait. He

grumbled at her and refused to help as she maneuvered him into his chair, combed his hair and brushed his teeth. When she took out clothes for him to wear, he rejected her choices. He folded his arms and ducked his head, anger etched in every line of his face.

Tom found her kneeling in front of the wheelchair, trying to put socks on Martin's cold feet. The old man kicked at her and swore under his breath. At least, she assumed it was swearing. She couldn't make out the words but his intent was clear.

"What's going on?" Tom asked.

"Dad's mad because I made him wait. Now he won't cooperate."

"Stop acting like a spoiled baby." Tom put his hand on Martin's shoulder and glared at him. "She wears herself out looking after you. If she wants to sleep in one morning, she's entitled."

Karen looked away, afraid she might blush or otherwise give away the fact that she hadn't exactly been sleeping.

"Go...away!" Martin shouted.

Tom took hold of her arm and pulled her up. "Come on, Karen. If he's going to act like that, he can just sit here in his pajamas."

"Tom. He'll get cold."

"It's ninety-five degrees outside. He won't get cold." He pulled her toward the door.

Once they were in the hallway, she jerked away from him. "What's wrong with you?" she demanded.

"I'm not going to stand by and watch him treat you like some hired servant and not say anything."

"He's a sick old man. He doesn't mean anything by it."

"He'd behave better if you made him."

"So now this is *my* fault?" Rage rose in her like lava, threatening to erupt all over both of them. How could she have believed last night that everything was all right between them, when nothing had changed? Tom still wanted her to choose between him and her father. He still refused to understand why he was asking too much. She balled her hands into fists, fighting the urge to beat against his chest. She glared at him, struggling for some way to express her feelings that didn't involve violence or swearing.

"I'm going to make some coffee," he said, and turned on his heels.

The fact that he'd walk away in the middle of an argument enraged her further, but short of running after him and dragging him back, she didn't know what to do. Instead, she headed across the hall and barged into Casey's room.

"Get up," she said, shaking her sleeping son.

"Wha—?" He opened one eye and looked up at her.

"I need you to get up and help Grandpa dress," she said.

"Why don't you do it?" he mumbled and rolled over, his back to her.

"Because I want you to." She jerked the covers off him. "Just do it. Now."

She left Casey's room and went into the kitchen. A fresh pot of coffee beckoned, but Tom was nowhere in sight. He'd left before she had the chance to confront him again about his boorish behavior.

She poured a cup of coffee and sat at the table, exhausted already and it wasn't even nine o'clock. The weight of unfinished business made her chest hurt. She hated fighting with Tom—hated it so much she usually gave in and did what he wanted. Saying what she felt was much harder than letting him have his way.

But years of swallowing words had left her feeling choked, and fearful there were some things that were too broken to fix.

Sunday afternoon, Casey found himself standing beneath a ladder, holding a section of gutter while his dad worked on connecting it to the eaves overhead. It was amazing, really, how his dad hadn't been in Grandpa's house twenty-four hours and he'd come up with a list of things that needed repairing or replacing. That said a lot about the kind of man his dad was. He was a man who fixed things. The kind of man who hated any kind of disorder or uncertainty.

Which was probably why he clashed with Casey so often. The way Casey saw it, the world was all about uncertainty. Instead of wearing yourself out trying to set everything and everybody straight, you were a lot better off taking things as they came and dealing with them the best you could.

"I talked to the counselors at school and they're going to let you take your finals the week before classes start this fall," his father said as he fit a new screw into the tip of the drill driver.

"What if I'm not home by then? Grandpa—" But his words were cut off by the scream of the drill as the screw bit into the sheet metal of the gutter.

"You'll be home by then," his dad answered when he'd shut off the drill. "You can't afford to miss any more school."

End of discussion, at least as far as Dad was concerned. But Casey had more to say on the subject. "I've been thinking. Maybe I could finish school online. They have this stuff called distance learning, where you study at your own pace."

"You don't study now, with your mom and I and all your teachers on your case. I'm supposed to believe you'll volunteer to do it on your own?"

"I don't mind studying if it's something that interests me. The teachers at school make everything so boring."

"I don't see how a computer is going to make math and history and English any less boring. Hand me another one of those screws."

Casey handed up the fastener. "We could try it."

Yeah, the subject matter would be the same in the online courses, but he liked the idea of being more in charge. For instance, he could decide whether to do English or math first, and how long he'd spend with each class, instead of having a schedule dictated by others.

"No. I don't see why I should pay for you to take special classes when there's a perfectly good high school not two miles from our house."

Casey could have argued that the high school wasn't all that good, but what was the point? Dad had made up his mind. He was always right.

The thing to do now was to wait and go to Mom with his plan. She at least considered his point of view. Maybe she could sway Dad to let him give this a try.

"I know you think I'm too hard on you, but it's because I know you can do better. And I know life will be easier for you in the long run if you apply yourself more." He leaned back and studied the gutter. "Does that look straight to you?"

"Yeah, it looks good." Casey didn't know what to say to the *apply yourself* remark. It was one of those clichés parents and teachers threw around, but what did it mean, exactly? If he preferred to focus on things that interested him, how was that not applying himself?

"Your mom says you've been a real help with your grandfather."

The change of subject caught him off guard. "Yeah, well, he cooperates a little better with me on some things. Maybe he's embarrassed because Mom's his daughter." It had freaked him out a little, the first time he'd helped the old man change clothes, or worse, when Grandpa wet his pants and Casey had to clean him up. He didn't do that so often anymore and besides, after the first time it had been sort of routine. He'd gotten into the habit of talking them both through it, making like it was no big deal.

"I'm not happy about the way you ran off without telling anyone, and without finishing school," Dad said. "But I'm glad you're a help to her."

Dad wasn't the type to go around handing out praise left and right, so having him acknowledge that his youngest had done something good for a change made Casey feel about a foot taller. "I'm glad I could help her, too."

"Good." Dad nodded, and climbed down the ladder. "That should do it. Now let's see about getting that porch light replaced."

"Right." One job done, time to move on to another. Casey would never understand this kind of methodical approach to life, but he guessed that was okay. He'd just do like he did with Grandpa—keep talking and keep moving along. It saved everybody from a lot of awkward moments that way.

CHAPTER 13

My heart is like a singing bird.
—*Christina Rosetti, "A Birthday"*

Karen returned from shopping to find Tom, Casey and Martin on the back porch, arguing. She followed the sound of raised voices and found the three of them gathered around the back steps, scowling at each other.

"What's going on here?" she asked.

"I'm trying to repair this broken light over the back steps," Tom said.

"Don't want...fixed," her father said, shaking his head.

"Why wouldn't you want it fixed?" Tom's voice was full of scorn. "Do you *want* everything to just fall down around your head?"

"Hurts...birds." Martin's chin jutted out and his eyes were dark and agitated.

"What? How the hell does the light hurt birds?"

"Re-flex." The old man shook his head. "Like mirror."

"I think what he means is, when the light's on, it

reflects on the glass on the sunporch and the birds think it's a mirror and fly into it," Casey said.

"You stay out of this," Tom snapped.

"Leave...him...alone!" Martin roared.

"He's my son, I'll—"

"Tom, please." Karen stepped between the two men and urged Tom into the house. Once inside, she pulled him into her bedroom and shut the door.

"What's going on?"

"I'm trying to help the old man and he picks a fight."

"It's his house. If he doesn't want the light fixed, leave it alone."

"It's his house, but you're living here. Not having a light over the back steps is unsafe."

"It's okay. I won't be here that much longer." She hoped. She had a feeling Tom's anger wasn't so much over the lack of a light as it was over her father not appreciating his efforts to help. That, and a continuation of the argument he and Karen had started this morning.

"You won't leave here soon enough to suit me," he said.

"I'm hoping by the end of the summer Dad will be able to look after himself. Or be able to manage with a housekeeper or other help a couple of days a week."

"I don't know why you didn't put him in a nursing home in the first place."

"He's my father. I couldn't do that."

He looked past her, toward where her dad sat on the other side of the wall. "Why not? He's an antisocial introvert, who relates to numbers, not people." His eyes met hers again. "You think I don't know how he's hurt you in the past? You can't expect me to be happy you're choosing to look after him, in spite of all that, when you could be home with your family."

When you could be home with me. If that's what he meant, then why didn't he say it that way? She ducked her head, blinking hard. She didn't know if the tears that threatened were because of Tom's outrage over her father's past neglect of her, or the way his words reminded her of those old hurts.

But since coming here, she'd discovered another side to her father. In the hours he'd spent teaching her about birds, she'd discovered a sensitive soul who appreciated beauty for beauty's sake. She'd thought birding was all about the numbers for him; this spiritual aspect had surprised her.

"He *is* introverted. And sometimes antisocial," she conceded. "But now, while he has to depend on me, is the best chance I'll ever have for us to be close." She struggled to find the words to make Tom understand why this was so important to her. "All my life, I've felt like…like I loved my father more than he loved me." She closed her eyes, squeezing back the tears that painful truth brought forth.

"Then you know how *I* feel."

The words floated on the top of her consciousness, like black oil spilled across a pristine lake—dark and ugly and shockingly out of place. She stopped breathing for a moment, stunned. "Wh-what do you mean?"

"I mean our marriage has been one-sided for years." The pain in his eyes forced her to take a step back. "Practically from the day I met you, I loved you," he continued. "I told myself it didn't matter if you didn't feel as strongly about me—that we'd grow into love. But it never happened."

"I *do* love you!" she cried. "You must know that."

"How am I supposed to know it? You never say it."

"I know." Why were three little words so hard to say? She could talk about loving chocolate or loving a song on the radio, but to say she loved her husband seemed too risky—as if saying the words out loud would tempt fate to take away everything she prized most. "It wasn't a word I heard a lot growing up. I took it for granted you *knew*."

He shook his head. "Be honest with me. When I asked you to marry me, did you love me then?"

She swallowed hard, a lie on the tip of her tongue. But pretending things were wonderful when they weren't hadn't made her any happier over the years. "I liked you, but I didn't have any idea what it meant to love someone that way. I only…I wanted to escape the life I had and I saw that you were the best chance I had at another one."

"That's what I thought." The disappointment in his voice made her stomach ache.

"Tom, wait, that doesn't mean I don't love you now."

But he had already stopped listening. He threw down his work gloves and pushed past her, out of the room. A few moments later, she heard the car start, gravel flying as he spun out of the driveway.

She sank down onto the bed, feeling as if the world had just tilted. His words hurt, as he must have meant them to. But his anger at her didn't wound nearly as deeply as her own recognition of how she'd let him down.

She thought she'd done a good job of hiding her true feelings in those early days of marriage. She'd wanted him to believe she returned his love for her right from the first, and she'd fooled herself into thinking she'd succeeded. Over the years, she had grown to truly cherish him, but she had never been one to express her emotions easily. She had thought it enough that she worked side by side with him at their business, kept their home and looked after his children. She hadn't seen the need for words, hadn't realized he felt their lack.

Oh God. Could it be she was truly her father's daughter, distanced from those she loved by the emotional reserve he had passed down to her?

How could she find her way across that chasm? How could she be anything other than the woman she was?

Casey couldn't believe his mom and dad could get so upset over a stupid porch light but then, he'd stopped trying to understand parents a long time ago. Whether it was the disagreement over the porch light or something else entirely, his dad ended up getting Mr. Wainwright to take him to the airport early.

His mom walked around the house for two days with red eyes, insisting she was "Fine," in a clipped tone of voice that made it obvious she was anything but. Grandpa retreated to his computer and threw a shoe at Lola again. The physical therapist didn't even blink; she picked up the shoe and threw it back, narrowly missing Grandpa's head. "You see how it feels, Mr. Engel," she said calmly. "Now let's try the arm raises again."

So when Uncle Del called and asked Casey to go fishing, he was thrilled. "Anything to get out of the nuthouse for a while," he said.

Del laughed. "I guess things haven't changed much since I was your age."

He picked Casey up early the next morning. "Is the dog coming?" Del asked as he loaded Casey's fishing gear into the back of the truck.

"Nah. I took her last time and she got bored in about five minutes. Drove me crazy whining and running around." Cradling an extra-large cup of coffee in both hands, he slumped against the passenger door of the truck and studied the road ahead through slitted eyes. The rising sun was a pinpoint of light glinting through the dark pines. "Where are we going?" he asked.

Del climbed in beside him and started the truck. "A place up on the river I know." He glanced at his nephew. "You're not a morning person, I guess."

"Nope." He slid farther down in the seat, knees braced against the dash.

"If you want to catch fish, you have to get up early."

"Why?"

"Because that's when the fish are biting. They wake up hungry and you want to be there with breakfast on your hook."

He wrinkled his nose. "I'd for sure sleep in if I knew breakfast was a bunch of worms."

"Nobody ever said fish were smart." He reached over and switched on the radio. A country singer mourned the girl who got away. Casey shut his eyes and tried to go back to sleep.

But the increasingly bright sun in his eyes and the coffee in his system overcame the last vestiges of sleep. By the time they turned onto the gravel track leading into the woods, he was sitting up straighter, and beginning to feel hungry. "You got anything to eat?" he asked.

"We'll have some breakfast when we get to the river," Del said.

He slowed the truck to a crawl as the road narrowed further. Casey grabbed hold of the door handle as they jostled over bumps and wallowed in ruts. Trees arched overhead, forming a canopy that shut out the sun. It looked like the setting for a creepy movie—*The Blair*

Witch Project or *Texas Chainsaw Massacre.* "How did you find this place?" he asked, wincing as they plunged into a deep rut.

"You just have to know the right people."

What kind of people? Casey wondered. Satan-worshippers? Bootleggers? Marijuana farmers? But before he could ask, they emerged onto an open bluff that overlooked the river. Del parked beneath an arched live oak and shut off the ignition. In the sudden stillness the only sounds were the pinging of the cooling engine and the trill of birdsong somewhere overhead.

"Where are we?" Casey asked.

"About five miles down from the power plant dam." Del opened the door and climbed out. "Grab that cooler and we'll head down to the river."

Casey picked up the cooler, which must have weighed about thirty pounds, while Del grabbed the poles, a tackle box and a faded blue backpack. He led the way down a steep path to a wide sandy beach beside the river. An old fire ring sat between two bleached cottonwood logs. Del dropped his gear beside one of the logs and stretched his arms over his head. "Don't you feel sorry for all the bastards stuck behind desks on a day like this?" he said.

"Yeah." Casey opened the cooler and stared at what must have been a case of beer on ice. He looked up at his uncle. "I thought you said you had food."

"It's in the pack." He grabbed a can of beer and popped the top. "Help yourself."

The pack held a foot-long submarine sandwich wrapped in wax paper, a pack of beef jerky and another of corn chips. "This is more like it," Casey said, unwrapping the sandwich.

While Casey ate, Del untangled lines and baited hooks. He handed one of the poles to Casey. "You ready to catch some fish?"

"Sure." He folded the wax paper over the remains of the sandwich and stashed it in the pack, then followed Del to the river.

Sunlight gilded the water to a bright copper color, the reflections of the cottonwoods and pines along the bank showing black in the still surface. "You want to cast over there by that old log." Del pointed across the water. "Let your hook rest almost on the bottom. Catfish are bottom feeders."

He managed to cast into the general area Del had indicated, then cranked the reel until the red and white bobber floated on the surface. "Now what?" he asked.

Del sat on the bank and leaned back against a tree trunk. "Now we wait."

They fell silent, the rising heat and stillness lulling them into a half doze. Casey focused on the red-and-white cork bobbing in the gentle current, allowing the rest of his vision to blur. Overhead a mockingbird ran through a repertoire of whistles and clicks, varying the calls for several minutes, then repeating the sequence again. Casey leaned forward, elbows on knees, and felt as if he was sinking into the soft sand of the riverbank, like a tree, rooted in place.

He decided all those people who studied yoga and consulted gurus and tried to learn how to meditate just needed to take up fishing. All those rednecks who spent every Saturday at the river, drinking beer and baiting hooks, probably never realized they were doing something so zen.

After half an hour or so, Del got a strike. He grabbed up the pole and began reeling it in, letting it out periodically, then taking it back up. He hauled in a good-sized catfish, hooking a finger through the gills and pulling it up on the bank. "That's a good three-pounder," he said, unhooking the fish and fastening it to the stringer, which he dropped in a deep pool farther down the bank.

"I'm not getting a thing," Casey said.

"Put a fresh worm on and try casting over to the left of that old stump."

He did as Del suggested and they both settled down to watch their poles once more. "Where's Mary Elisabeth today?" Casey asked.

"She's working." Del winked. "My advice is to always find a woman with a good job. If she has her own money, she won't be spending yours, and you can borrow from her if you need to."

"I thought the idea was for the man to support the woman," Casey said.

"You're behind the times, son. Women these days like to be independent. I say we should let them."

"Then what's to keep them from running off with some rich guy?" Personally, he thought Mary Elisabeth could probably have any man she wanted, so why had she picked Uncle Del?

"Because a rich man wouldn't really need them." He sat up straighter. "Women—most of 'em anyway—like to be needed. They'll devote themselves to a man who needs rescuing from himself."

"Why would they do that?"

Del shrugged. "Who knows? But it's true. You take your mama. She hadn't hardly set foot in this place in twenty years and the minute she heard the old man was sick, she rushed down here to look after him."

"But he's her father. That's different from a romantic relationship."

"Not that different. Trust me. Women want a man who needs them. That whole nurturing thing is in their genes."

Casey didn't think this philosophy painted either men or women in a very flattering light, but he kept this opinion to himself.

"So what's going on at the nuthouse?" Del asked. "Dad giving you a hard time?"

"He's giving everybody a hard time. But I don't blame him. I'd be ornery, too, if I was stuck in a wheelchair."

"Hmph. My dad would find something to complain about if he was a millionaire who'd just won a marathon." He looked out across the river again. "What about your dad? He have a good visit?"

Casey shifted. His mom would probably walk across hot coals before she'd tell anyone—much less her brother—about her troubles, but Casey wasn't as reticent. "Not really. He and Mom had a fight and he left early."

"Oh? What were they fighting about?"

He dug a groove in the sand with the heel of his shoe. "I don't know. I think maybe he wants her back in Denver and she feels like she needs to stay here."

Del looked up at the sky. "That's my sister. Always trying to make everybody happy and making herself miserable." He picked up his empty beer can and shook it, then crumpled it. "Time for a refill." He wedged his pole between two rocks, then stood and lumbered over to the cooler.

Casey reeled his pole in, saw the worm had been stolen, and set about impaling another one on the hook. He had just cast again when Del returned. "Here." He tapped Casey on the shoulder with a beer. "Drink up."

Casey took the beer without comment and cracked it open. It tasted good going down, so cold it made the back of his throat ache.

"I'm not trying to be hard on your mom," Del said as

he settled back against the tree trunk once more and opened a beer. "She's a good woman. Probably too good. She's got it into her head that if she does right by the old man, looking after him and everything, he's going to appreciate it. I'm here to tell you, it ain't gonna happen."

"What makes you say that? "

Del looked at him a long moment, as if trying to decide how much to share with his nephew. "Martin Engel cares more for a bunch of birds with funny names than he ever did for his own family," he said after a moment. "I could have been the worst juvenile delinquent in the history of Tipton, or the class valedictorian, and it wouldn't have made a bit of difference to him, as long as I didn't interfere with his plans to fly to Africa or spend two weeks in the Galapagos trying to see the Blue-footed Booby or whatever."

He spoke the words matter-of-factly, but the lines on either side of his jaw deepened, and his eyes reflected bitterness.

"I don't know." Casey wedged his rod between his feet and leaned back on his elbows. "I think he would have cared."

Del shook his head. "I've known him a lot longer than you have. I'm his son and every time I walk into that house, it's like I'm a stranger. I bet he couldn't tell you today what's going on in my life."

"I bet he could. He pays attention to stuff." Casey

raised up and drained the last of the beer, then reached for another. "I think he has really deep feelings about stuff. He's just one of those people who doesn't know how to show his emotions. Like…like he never learned how, or something."

"What makes you think that?"

He shrugged. "I don't know, just…when he looks at birds, the way he talks about them…for him they're like poetry, or music. Something so beautiful and special…I don't think somebody with no feelings would see them that way."

"Maybe he's like that with you. He isn't that way with me. Hey, looks like you got a bite."

They began catching fish in earnest, then. In between baiting hooks and casting, Casey drank more beer. He began to feel a pleasant buzz. This is how life should be—no hassles, no worries. Just take life as it comes….

Karen wandered restlessly about the house. Dad was asleep, worn out from his morning therapy appointment. Del had picked up Casey hours ago and taken him God knows where. Fishing, he'd said. Something they both loved. Something she hoped would keep them out of trouble.

She took out her notebook and consulted her list. There must be something on here that would occupy her, at least for a little while. But every item she'd written down was neatly crossed through. Tasks completed.

She ripped out the page, crumpled it, and tossed it toward the trash. It bounced off the side of the can and rolled under the sofa. She let it lie, half-afraid if she lay down on the floor to retrieve the paper, she'd stay there, weeping, until Casey came home and found her.

She stopped in front of the phone, staring at the silent receiver, willing it to ring. If only Tom would call her. They could talk. Find a way around this horrible silence between them.

She shook her head and turned away. And what would she say? *I want to be different. I want to be the wife you want, but I don't know if I have that in me.*

Is it so wrong for me to want you to love me in spite of everything I'm not?

She passed her bedroom and heard a snuffling noise from beside the bed. Investigating, she found Sadie lying on the rug. At first, she thought the dog had one of the rawhide chew toys Casey had bought her, but as she drew closer, she recognized one of a pair of leather sandals she'd bought for herself on her recent shopping trip with Casey.

"Sadie!" she shouted.

The dog jumped up and attempted to dive under the bed, but she was too large. So she simply lay there, her head shoved under the bedspread, the rest of her sticking out. It would have been comical if Karen hadn't been so furious.

She grabbed the dog's collar and dragged her out, gathering up the mangled shoe with her free hand. "Look what you did," she said, shaking the shoe in the dog's face. "These were brand-new. How could you?"

Sadie's eyes rolled upward and she attempted to duck her head. Karen could have sworn the dog's bottom lip trembled. The dog began to shake, and whimper pitifully.

"Stop that." Karen released her hold on the collar. "I'm not going to beat you. What kind of a person do you think I am?"

The kind of person who couldn't tell her husband she loved him. The kind of person who wasn't even sure what love meant anymore.

Sadie whined and shoved at Karen's hand, her nose cold and damp, an icy jolt to the senses. Karen felt hot tears slide down her cheeks and dropped to her knees beside the dog.

Sadie gently licked Karen's cheek, and nudged her hand again. She stared into Karen's face, eyes filled with concern. When was the last time anyone had cared so much what she, Karen, was feeling? Was that because no one cared, or because she was so careful to hide her emotions from others? She had spent so many years being the strong, practical one in any group, she'd forgotten what it meant to be vulnerable.

Sadie moved closer, into Karen's lap, and licked harder at the tears, her whines more insistent. Karen put her arms around the dog, surprised at how comforting hugging the furry beast could be. "I'm a mess," she said out loud.

Sadie whimpered, whether in agreement or sympathy Karen didn't know. Karen hugged her more tightly. "We women have to stick together," she said. "We're outnumbered in this household."

The dog's tail thumped hard against the floor, a steady rhythm. Like a heartbeat.

Karen laid her head alongside the animal's soft side. "I never had a dog before," she said. "So I'm new at this whole relating to animals thing. Then again, I haven't done such a great job relating to people." She drew back, and looked into the dog's soft, understanding eyes. "Maybe you can teach me a few things, huh girl?"

Sadie barked and wagged her tail more wildly. Karen shut her eyes, squeezing back more tears. How pitiful was it to be over forty years old, and taking lessons in love from a stray dog?

But she had to start somewhere. And she could trust Sadie not to judge her efforts too harshly. If only she could show the same compassion to herself.

Casey thought he must have fallen asleep. The next thing he knew, Del was standing over him, nudging him with the toe of his boot. "Wake up, boy. Time to head back to the house." He held up the string of fish. "We'll get Mary Elisabeth to cook us up a mess of catfish."

Casey shoved into a sitting position, then fell back, the world spinning crazily. He groaned. Dell's face loomed closer, distorted, like the view in a shiny hubcap. "You're not drunk, are you?"

"Nah, I'm not drunk." He sat up more slowly this time, steadying himself with one hand on the ground. "I jus' need to wake up."

"Well, come on. Mary Elisabeth will be home from work soon. She and your mom will be wondering where we disappeared to."

Somehow he managed to stand and carry the now-empty cooler up the slope to the truck. Once there, he slumped in the seat and closed his eyes. "You okay?" Del asked. "You're looking kind of green. I don't want you throwing up in my truck."

"I'm fine." He turned his face to the window, the cool glass against his cheek.

When Del started the car, Casey aimed the air-conditioning vent toward him. The cold air revived him some, and he sat up straighter. "Thanks for inviting me to come with you today," he said. "I had a great time."

"No problem. You're not bad company. You want to stay for supper?"

He was tempted, if only to see Mary Elisabeth, but decided against it. "I'd better get home. Help with Grandpa."

"It's your funeral."

CHAPTER 14

No bird soars too high if he soars with his
own wings.
—*William Blake*, The Marriage of Heaven
and Hell

Del dropped Casey off in front of Grandpa's house, then drove over to his trailer next door. Casey climbed the steps to the front door, holding on to the railing for support. Maybe he shouldn't have had those last few beers. Or had more to eat than part of a sub sandwich for breakfast.

He was hoping he could slip into his bedroom without being seen, but Mom met him at the door. "How was your fishing trip?" she asked. "Did you catch anything?"

"A few. Mary Elisabeth's going to cook them." But the words came out jumbled, more like "Few. Marliz'beth's gonna cook 'em."

Mom's eyes widened. "Casey Neil MacBride, are you drunk?"

"Nah. Only had a few." He tried to push past her, but her hand around his forearm was like a blood pressure cuff pumped up to full pressure. When did Mom get so strong?

"What did you have to drink?" she asked.

"Jus' beer." He blinked, trying to steady his vision. When he looked straight ahead, her hairline swam into view. Hey, he was taller than her now. Sweet.

"Del gave you beer?" Her voice rose to a squeak. She still had a hold of him, fingers digging into his skin. He wanted to ask her to let go, but all of a sudden he was feeling a little queasy. He didn't want to risk opening his mouth.

"How many did you have?" she asked.

He shrugged. They'd been talking and drinking and fishing. He hadn't counted. All he knew was the cooler was full when they started and empty when they headed home.

"So many you can't remember." She released his arm with a shake. "Go to your room. I don't want to see you again until morning. And I hope you have a hell of a hangover."

He knew he should apologize to her for coming home in this condition, but all he could manage was a groan. His stomach rolled and churned, like a restless sleeper. He lunged past her, down the hall and toward the bathroom.

He almost made it. Instead, he ended up on his knees, puking up his guts just outside the bathroom door.

His mother loomed over him again. "You clean that up, then go to bed."

He looked up at her through bleary eyes. From this angle she looked about six feet tall. "What are you gonna do?"

"I'm going next door to give your uncle a piece of my mind."

He nodded, and used the wall to climb back to a standing position. The stench of vomited beer almost made him heave again. He edged around it and found a couple of old towels in the back of the linen closet. Being stuck here cleaning puke wasn't the very worst thing he could imagine doing right now.

The worst thing was being Uncle Del when his mom lit into him.

Karen had to grant her brother one thing: the man wasn't dumb. He must have known how furious she'd be with him, so he hadn't stayed around his place long after dropping off his nephew. He'd probably gone to Mary Elisabeth's or to one of his no-account friends who'd be sure to take him in. She stood on the steps of his trailer and stared at the empty carport where his truck usually sat. Cold chills overtook her as she realized not only had he gotten her underage son drunk, he'd driven him home while Del himself was almost certainly feeling no pain.

She sat down on the top step and hugged her arms

around her knees. In a minute she'd go back and check on Casey, make sure he wasn't still vomiting or blacked out or anything.

"Thief! Thief! Thief!" The sharp cry of a Blue Jay drew her attention and she looked up to see one eyeing her from the top of the crepe myrtle bush beside the steps. It turned its head and fixed one black-rimmed eye on her and fluffed its feathers. *"Thief! Thief! Thief!"* it repeated.

"Do you know the thief who stole my little boy and replaced him with…with that drunken man throwing up in my hall?" she muttered. Casey was taller than her now, and the arm she'd grabbed was wiry with muscle. That as much as seeing his eyes glazed and hearing his slurred speech had frightened her. Somewhere in the last few weeks or months he'd transformed. He wasn't her child anymore. He was his own, independent person, one with secrets and dreams and dirty deeds she'd never know about. She'd known this would happen. She'd already been through it with Matt, but she had imagined she could hold on to Casey, her dreamer, a little longer.

One afternoon with Del and he'd gotten away from her.

She stood and headed back toward the house. Tomorrow, she'd deal with Del. Right now, she needed to find the aspirin, and check on her wayward boy.

The next morning, Karen was over at Del's as soon as she saw his truck pull into the driveway. She intercepted him as he inserted the key in his front door. "We need to talk," she said.

He gave her a sour look. "Not now, sis. I'm busy."

"You're not too busy to talk to me." She followed him into the house and stood between him and the bedroom door, in case he got any ideas about retreating there and locking her out.

"You're mad about Casey." He tossed his truck keys onto the kitchen counter, wincing when they clattered against the tile top. He looked about as rough as he must have felt—his hair needed combing and whiskers stuck out a quarter inch all over his chin.

"You took a sixteen-year-old and got him drunk!"

"Hey, I didn't pour the beer down his throat. And what's wrong with him having a couple of beers? It didn't hurt anything."

"It was more than a couple. He was sick all over the floor as soon as he got home."

Del made a face. "He'll learn to hold his liquor better when he gets older."

"I don't want him learning that kind of lesson."

"Learning that lesson is part of growing up. Deal with it." He sank onto the sofa and rubbed his temples. "Now that we've had this little discussion, could you leave me alone?"

"No, I won't leave you alone. We're not through talking." Anger and frustration pressed at the back of her throat, sending words rushing out of her. "You may think it's all right to waste your life sponging off other people and playing the charming rogue, but I want better for my son. I don't want him to be like you."

Del narrowed his eyes. "Yeah, I know. You want to make him into some uptight worker bee, someone who keeps his nose clean and *contributes* to society and does his mama proud. It's really all about you, isn't it?"

"It's not about me." What was wrong with wanting to be proud of her child? Or wanting to know that he was financially secure and successful? "It's about Casey growing up to be the best he can be." All he needed was a way to channel his talents, something that would interest him enough for him to focus. He wasn't going to find that sitting on a riverbank, drinking beer with his uncle.

"Then quit trying to force him into a mold you've made for him. He's his own person." Del sat forward, his gaze burning into her, his voice a menacing growl that made her take a step back. "He's more like me than you'll ever admit. The sooner you accept that and let him be, the happier we'll all be."

"I won't accept it." She pushed back a wave of panic and took a deep breath. "I'm his mother. My job is to help shape his life. There's nothing wrong with that."

"There is if you can't be happy with him the way he is. Keep trying to make him into what he's not and you'll drive him away for sure."

"That's not true."

"What would you know about it? You've spent your whole life trying to be whatever anyone wanted you to be. And it didn't make you any happier, did it?" He sagged back on the sofa and closed his eyes. "Get out of my house. Before I throw you out."

She ran from the trailer, gasping for fresh air, trying to clear the ugly images his uglier words had conjured: of Casey growing up to be like Del, and of herself as some ever-changing chameleon, trying to please people—her father, Tom, even her boys—who could never be pleased.

The idea made her cold. Was she that way? Maybe, but was it so bad—to want to make the people you loved happy?

But what about making yourself happy? The voice in her head was quiet, but clear, and the question repeated itself over and over, a mantra she couldn't shake.

Karen had calmed down some by the time Casey shuffled out of his room shortly before noon. When he saw her, he ducked his head. "You don't have to say anything. I know I messed up."

"Good. Then you've saved me the trouble of hauling out my lecture on the evils of underage drinking." She folded her arms across her chest and studied him. He was still wearing the clothes he'd had on yesterday, and his hair stuck out in all directions. He looked like some homeless person—or a typical teenage boy, depending on your perspective. "I don't want you going off alone with Uncle Del anymore."

"Aw, Mom." He frowned at her. "This wasn't his fault."

"He brought the beer. And he didn't do anything to stop you from drinking it. If I know Del, he probably encouraged it."

The guilty look on his face told her she was right. "He's supposed to be the adult," she continued. "But he certainly didn't act like one."

He shoved his hands in his pockets. "I like Uncle Del because he doesn't treat me like a kid."

"But you are a kid." She looked him up and down. "Not a little one, but you're not an adult yet, either. And I don't even want to think what could have happened if there'd been an accident on the way home. Del certainly wasn't in any shape to be driving."

"But nothing happened."

"Nothing happened this time. I'm not willing to risk a second chance. I've already spoken to Del. He knows how I feel."

He shuffled past her to the refrigerator, where he took out a Coke. "So what's up with Dad? Why'd he leave early?"

She winced. Leave it to Casey to change the subject to something even more upsetting to talk about. Her first instinct was to try to get the conversation back on track, but that was the easy way out. The one that didn't require her to be honest about her feelings.

She took a deep breath. How much harm had been done already by never revealing how she truly felt? "He thinks I should put Grandpa in a nursing home and come back to Denver right away. I'm not ready to do that yet." That wasn't the only problem, but the only one she was willing to share with Casey.

"Uncle Del thinks Grandpa doesn't care about anyone or anything but birds."

She sat at the table and stared at her folded hands. "Sometimes it seems that way."

Casey sat across from her, long legs stretched out in front of him. "I told him I think Grandpa cares about a lot of things. He's just not one to show his feelings." He took a swig of soda. "Maybe he doesn't know how to show them."

She wanted to hug him then, but the fear she'd break down altogether if she did so held her back. "Emotions can be scary things," she said, choosing her words carefully. "People have different ways of showing them."

He nodded. "I know." He leaned over and awkwardly patted her hand. "Dad will come around. He just misses you a lot. When you're back home again, he'll understand you couldn't just run out on Grandpa."

She nodded, unable to force any words past the knot in her throat. If only it were that simple.

Casey stood and tossed the empty Coke can into the trash. "I think I'll take a shower."

She watched him go, thinking about the things each generation passed on to the next. Casey had her hair and her nose, and his father's eyes and chin. But he had an emotional openness she'd never known, and a tolerance for others' differences his father certainly didn't possess. Something outside of them had shaped his character. It gave her hope he'd avoid the mistakes she'd made.

Mistakes she was still making. She looked back toward her father's office. He was in there, exchanging e-mails with his birding friends and making plans for his next expedition. She hoped before too many weeks he'd be able to look after himself, or at least get by with the help of a housekeeper and maybe a visiting nurse.

She stared at the closed door of the office. All these weeks she and her father had tiptoed around each other's feelings. They talked, but never said anything too important. She'd been waiting for him to make the first move—for him to apologize for his distance over the years, to thank her for caring for him now.

She'd been waiting for him to tell her he loved her. As if a man who'd been silent about his feelings for seventy years would suddenly find words to express them.

Oh, she was her father's daughter all right—keeping her emotions locked away where no one could ridicule or reject them. Which left her like a child standing outside the door, waiting to be invited into the party, but too afraid to ring the bell.

No one was going to ring it for her. No one could break this family curse but her. On shaking legs, she stood and walked down the hall, to the door of the study. She waited a long moment, then raised her hand and knocked, holding her breath as she listened for an answer.

CHAPTER 15

And what is a bird without its song? Do we not wait for the stranger to speak? It seems to me that I do not know a bird till I have heard its voice; then I come nearer it at once, and it possesses a human interest to me.
—John Burroughs, Birds and Bees, Sharp Eyes and Other Papers

"In!" Martin commanded. His voice was much stronger now, though he still favored one- or two-word sentences, the minimum number of words to make himself understood.

Karen entered and dragged a chair around to sit in front of him. "We need to talk," she said.

He looked at her, eyes alert, like a crow waiting to snatch the fragments of a picnic lunch. She smoothed her palms down her thighs. "When you had your stroke, and Mom asked me to come look after you, I didn't want to at first."

He nodded, expression unchanging, as if this information wasn't new or surprising.

"But then I thought, I should do it. Because… because you're my dad and…and because I thought this might be our last chance to really get to know each other." She looked at him, silently pleading with him to help her out here. Meet her halfway. "You were gone so much when I was growing up. And even when you were home, I—I never felt like I was very important to you." Her voice broke on the last words, and she choked back a sob. *Oh God, please don't let me break down.*

She snatched a tissue from the box on the desk and blew her nose loudly, then took a deep breath, determined to get through this. "You were the one person I most wanted to love me. To *like* me. But I never felt that. So I thought, this is our second chance. But now that I'm here—all these weeks…" She shook her head. "Has it made any difference at all?"

He looked away from her, down at his lap, his expression as unreadable as ever. Her spirits sank and she bit her lip to keep from crying out, drawing blood, which tasted like the tears she refused to shed. They were a pair, weren't they? Crippled by reticence, hearts encased in protective shells that distanced them from everyone else, even each other.

His hand trembled as he reached for her, but his grasp was surprisingly strong. "I'm…sorry," he said, his voice gruff. "I...care. Took...for granted...that you knew." He squeezed harder. "I don't know how...to say things...right." He shrugged, and met her gaze, his eyes glossy with tears. "This is how...I am...too old...to change."

"I know." She leaned forward to embrace him, the strength of his arm around her conveying as much as his words. "I just had to hear it. Once." She patted his back, and rested her head on his shoulder, his bones feeling fragile as a bird's against her cheek. "It's all right now."

She'd wanted more, but would take what she could get. He was probably right, that he was too old to change. But was she? Was she too old to find a way to break this family curse that held her feelings hostage behind brittle walls?

After a long moment, Martin pushed away. He picked up his binoculars from the desk and rolled his chair to the picture window. He raised the glasses to his eyes and scanned the scene outside, looking for birds.

Looking away from her. Always looking away.

The intense exchange with Karen left Martin drained. He retired to his room and lay down, pondering the rare moment of intimacy with his offspring. He was filled with the same feeling of privilege and elation he had when he had seen a rare bird. Karen was like a bird in that respect—he had moments when he felt he truly saw her and understood her, but these moments were all too fleeting.

As the air-conditioning hummed against the late afternoon heat, he drifted to sleep, and dreamed of the jungle. The air was thick and heavy in his lungs, his vision obscured by tangled vines and leaning tree trunks. A bird darted past, and his heart pounded as he recognized the chunky silhouette of the Brown-chested Barbet.

He took a step forward to follow, and found himself falling through the air. He opened his mouth to scream, but no sound emerged. No one would know when he died here, alone.

But as the ground rushed toward him, he was suddenly caught, as if at the end of a string, and he began to rise again, soaring under his own power. He was flying! He had no wings, only his arms extended in the manner of a child playing airplane. Yet miraculously, he was held upright, floating on a current of warm air.

Exhilarated, he searched for the Barbet and spotted it ahead. It seemed almost to be waiting for him, hovering in the air. He zoomed after it, coming so close he could see the feathers lying along its back like scales. Then it raced ahead.

Effortlessly, he pursued it, swooping and gliding, laughing out loud with joy. He had never felt so weightless. So free. Warm air blew his hair back from his face and pressed his clothes against his body. His fingertips brushed the velvet petals of orchids, and he breathed deeply of their rich perfume. A pair of long-tailed Capuchin monkeys eyed him curiously from their perches in the trees.

The Barbet flew ahead, always just out of reach. Martin followed, not caring where they ended up, delighting in the moment. Why had he never done this before?

The Barbet landed on the end of a branch and began to preen, thick beak ruffling its wing feathers. Martin slowed, and readied for a landing beside the bird, instinctively knowing how to bank and aim for the branch. He stretched out his legs, ready to make contact, some small part of his brain wondering if the narrow limb would really support his weight.

He woke with a start, eyes opened wide to the sun streaming through his bedroom window. He shut them again, willing the dream world to return, but the orange glow of sunlight against his closed eyelids told him sleep had escaped him. He spread his arms, remembering the feel of flight, but his left side remained leaden and unresponsive.

Tears of frustration spilled from beneath his closed eyelids and rolled down his cheeks, wetting the pillow. After the freedom of flight, he felt imprisoned in his damaged body, bereft as a child who has lost the only source of happiness in his world.

* * *

Casey decided he'd better try to make it up to his mom for coming home drunk the other day, so he offered to finish mowing the backyard.

"You can't," she said. "There's a Killdeer sitting on a nest near the pond."

"Not anymore. Grandpa and I checked it out the other day. The babies are grown and flew away."

"Already?" She checked the calendar. "It's only been two weeks."

He shrugged. "I guess that's all it takes with birds." He slipped on his sunglasses. "Anyway, think I'll go mow."

"Be careful. It looks like a storm is coming up."

He glanced out the window. The sky did look dark in the distance. "I'll have time to finish before it gets bad," he said.

"Okay." She looked a little dazed. Maybe she was shocked he'd volunteer to do a chore. So maybe he wasn't that crazy about work—who was? That didn't mean he couldn't do it when he needed to.

He was filling the gas tank on the mower when Mary Elisabeth wandered over from Uncle Del's trailer. "Hey," she said, stopping beside the mower.

"Hey yourself." He grinned at her. She was wearing Daisy Dukes and a sleeveless denim shirt that tied under her breasts. The ring in her navel glittered in the sunlight. "What's up?"

"I heard about your fishing trip," she said.

He flushed. "Yeah, Mom's pissed at Uncle Del. Nothing new about that, I guess."

"Smart people do dumb things sometimes."

"Yeah." He set the gas can aside and screwed the cap back on the mower. "I told her Uncle Del didn't mean any harm."

She poked him in the shoulder. "I'm not talking about Del, I'm talking about you."

He stared at her. "You think I'm smart?"

Her smile could have melted chocolate. "Of course you're smart. I bet you make As in school."

He made a face. "You'd lose that bet. I hate school."

"Why? Because it's boring?"

He nodded. "Yeah."

"Just suck it up and get through it." She shrugged. "You have to do that sometimes."

"I don't see why. I mean, why not do what makes you happy, as long as you're not hurting anybody?" He figured she could understand that philosophy.

"But sometimes you end up hurting yourself." Her expression was serious now. If not for the whole short-shorts and navel ring thing, she might have looked like somebody's mom. "If you don't finish school, how are you going to support yourself? And what if you meet someone and want to get married and have a family? Then you'll need to support them."

"Whoa. I'm not thinking about supporting anybody right now. I can deal with that when the time comes."

What was it with women? Did they all have this mom-thing inside their brains? Something tripped a switch and this perfect mom-speech came out? It was wild.

"The choices you make do affect your future," she said. "Realizing that is part of growing up."

Was she saying she didn't think he was grown up? He stared at the ground between his feet. "I guess sometimes it's more fun to stay a kid."

"Yeah, we all feel that way sometimes."

She nudged his shoulder again, the smile back in place, and he relaxed a little. "Do you feel that way?" he asked.

"Oh, sure. I bet even your mom feels that way every once in a while."

"Mom? No way. She was born grown up."

She laughed. "No, I bet she sometimes thinks of ditching all the responsibility and just doing what she wants for a change."

This idea was both frightening and intriguing. His mom, a free spirit? He shook his head. "If that's the way she feels, why doesn't she?"

She leaned against the mower and crossed her arms under her breasts. "Maybe because it's too scary. Or maybe because she loves you all too much not to keep looking after you."

He fiddled with the gearshift knob on the mower. "Mom's not one for a lot of mushy talk. I mean, I know she cares about us, she just doesn't say it all the time. Not like some women. I have this one friend, Joe—his mom hugs and kisses him and tells him she loves him every time he leaves the house. Like he's going to forget or something." He shuddered. "I always feel kind of embarrassed for him."

"Some people are more expressive than others," Mary Elisabeth said. "It doesn't mean they love any more, they just like to talk about it, I guess."

"If something's the truth, I don't think you have to keep saying it."

"Yeah, but you should say it every once in a while, just to remind yourself."

He fiddled with the gearshift some more, watching her through half-closed eyes. He got the feeling something was on her mind. "So did you just feel like giving me a bunch of advice today?"

"No, silly." She looked at him sideways, almost shyly. "Actually, I came to say goodbye."

"Goodbye?" His heart hammered in his chest. "Are you going away?"

"Yeah. My sister in California invited me to come out and stay with her for a while. I think I'm going to do it."

"What about Del?"

"Oh, he'll be all right. A man like him never goes long without a woman around."

The casualness of her attitude bothered him. He'd thought she really cared about his uncle. "Aren't you going to miss him?" Wasn't Del going to miss *her*?

"Sometimes. We had fun." She straightened. "But I'm

not ready to get serious about someone right now. And he isn't, either, which I guess is why things worked for us. Maybe I'll hook up with a surfer dude in California."

Too bad Casey wasn't a surfer. And about ten years older.

"So what about you?" she asked. "Are you going back to Denver soon?"

"At the end of the summer, I guess." He looked toward the house. "Grandpa's doing better."

"He is. I'm glad. He's an interesting guy."

"I guess he is." He glanced at her. "Most people are interesting, if you get to know them a little."

"I like the way you think." She brushed off her shorts. "I guess I'd better be going. I told my sister I'd leave in the morning and I still have packing to do."

"Thanks for stopping by." He wiped his hand on his jeans and offered it to her. "Have a good trip."

"You, too." She took his hand and held it in both of hers. "Remember, you can get through anything if you have to. Even boring school."

"Yeah." Though he still wasn't so sure about that.

She surprised him then, by tugging him toward her and stretching up to kiss his cheek. Then she was gone, walking across the yard without looking back.

He put his hand to his face, still feeling the soft brush of her lips against his skin, her flowery perfume filling his nostrils. He felt warm all over, and as if his feet might not be touching the ground.

Wow.

* * *

Karen watched Casey and Mary Elisabeth out the kitchen window. The young woman had already stopped by the house and said her goodbyes. Karen wondered how Casey would take the news of her leaving. She was pretty sure her son had a crush on his uncle's girlfriend. What teenage boy wouldn't? Mary Elisabeth looked like a *Playboy* centerfold come to life.

Karen was surprised by how much she was going to miss the younger woman. Mary Elisabeth was the kind of person who calmed the atmosphere just by being in a room. Dad was less argumentative when she was around, and even Del could be pleasant under the influence of his younger girlfriend.

She envied Mary Elisabeth, too, for going off on her own, the way Karen never had the courage to do. She'd had big dreams of traveling and making her way in the world, but in the end she'd stayed right here in Tipton after graduation, leaving only when Tom had provided the opportunity.

Now here she was, her children almost grown, her husband angry with her for not giving more of herself to him, her brother disgusted with her because she'd made the mistake of thinking life should be neat and orderly and people's reactions predictable.

She had done one thing right, at least. She and Dad understood each other now. No, he hadn't been the perfect childhood father she'd wanted, but neither had he been the horrible one her selective memory some-times made him out to be. He'd done the best he could with what he had in him. Something she'd tried to do for her boys, too.

She left the kitchen and wandered down the hall to Martin's study. She was surprised to find him, not at the computer as she'd expected, but at the window.

"Storm coming," he said. Every day his speech was clearer, though he was still unable to use his left limbs.

"We could use rain," she said. "The weatherman said this is the remnants of a tropical depression from South America."

"Birds get caught in big storms," he said. "Blown off course." He looked at her, his expression charged with an-ticipation. "Chance to see…birds not seen here…be-fore."

"Maybe we'll both have some to add to our lists," she said, though she doubted there was a bird anywhere near here that her father hadn't already seen. "Casey said the Killdeer chicks are grown and gone already," she added.

He turned from the window again. "They have to grow up fast," he said. "Be ready for…migration."

She picked up a paperweight from the edge of the desk, then set it down again. "What do the adult birds—the mothers—do after the chicks are grown?" she asked. "Do they stay with them or what?"

His forehead wrinkled as he pondered the question. "They go on...being birds." He shrugged. "That's all."

She nodded, the skin on the back of her neck tingling as the idea took hold. Was she like the Killdeer? Could she go on being Karen? Did that mean staying the same, or trying something different?

She'd never thought much about her future—what life would be like when the boys were grown, and beyond that even, to when she could retire from the landscaping business. Maybe she hadn't wanted to think about a time that seemed so scary. She'd spent her whole life being busy, catering to those around her. What would she do with herself when they no longer needed her?

"Dad, can I ask you a question?"

He looked at her, waiting.

"Why birding? What about it made it worth leaving your family, traveling all over the world and enduring so many hardships?" She looked at the awards arrayed on his wall. Surely he hadn't devoted so much of his life to acquiring these pieces of paper. She looked back at him. "I've read all the articles written about you in birding magazines, about how you've walked across deserts and stood in the cold for hours and gotten up in the middle of the night—all to see birds. Why would anyone do that?"

He frowned, the lines on his forehead deepening. He opened his mouth, then closed it again, and moved to the computer and began typing.

She came to stand beside him, and watched the words form on the screen.

I don't know how to explain.

"Try. I want to understand."

When you've waited all night and endured the heat or cold, and finally you see the bird you've been seeking—the feeling is so beautiful, so sweet.... You know then that you've done the right thing. The thing your soul needs you to do.

She blinked, and read the words on the screen again, letting them soak in. *The thing your soul needs you to do*. What did her soul need her to do? Was this restlessness she felt of late a sign that she needed to make changes in her life—find a new job? Travel to another country? Leave Tom and start over with someone else? Or by herself?

She hugged her arms across her chest, as if she could ward off the psychic chill that swept through her. She didn't know if she was as strong as her father, who endured great hardships in hopes of some elusive reward. She didn't think she was as brave as Mary Elisabeth, willing to uproot herself and move across the country for the sake of trying something different. And she wasn't as carefree as Casey, who trusted the future to take care of itself.

That brought her back to the mother Killdeer, and the idea of being Karen. Who was this mysterious woman, and how could she discover her? How could she find the thing her soul needed her to do?

CHAPTER 16

If life is, as some hold it to be, a vast melancholy ocean over which ships more or less sorrow-laden continually pass, yet there lie here and there upon it isles of consolation on to which we may step out and for a time forget the winds and waves. One of these we may call Bird-isle—the island of watching and being entertained by the habits and humours of birds.
—Edmund Selous, Bird Watching

The storm hit while they were eating supper, rain sounding like gravel against the windows, the tops of the pine trees bent like heavy stalks of wheat in the on-slaught. Before he went to bed that night, Martin persuaded Casey to help him position the spotting scope. "Tomorrow…we'll see what blew in on the wind," he explained. He hadn't much hope of adding to his list, but he might be able to point out something interesting for Karen or Casey to add to their lists.

He also had the boy open the window a couple of

inches. He lay in bed later with the lights out, breathing in the green smell of wet pine and fertile loam. It reminded him a little of the jungles of Brazil, which smelled of wet and growing things, and the pungent richness of decay.

He fell asleep to the drum of rain cascading off the eaves, which became the steady cadence of dew dripping from the leaves of rubber trees.

A familiar cry assailed him, and the Brown-chested Barbet flitted into view. It landed on a branch above his head and cocked one eye at him, as if to pose a question or a challenge. Then with a soft flutter of wings it rose into the air and flew away.

Martin spread his arms and stood on tiptoe, a fledgling eager to join in the flight. But gravity held him firmly to the ground. No longer could he fly among the treetops with the birds, though the memory of how that freedom had felt stayed with him, like the scent of a loved one clinging to his clothes though they were long departed.

He clenched his fists and a keening cry of mourning tore from his throat. Why was he trapped here this way, immobile and useless, the things he loved most out of his reach in the treetops?

He woke before dawn, irritable and unrested. The rain had stopped and the sky had lightened to an ashy gray. Restless, he maneuvered from the bed to the wheelchair and rolled to the window, where he checked the spotting scope. Already, birds were awake, scratching for worms and insects in the rain-softened soil, bathing in puddles that formed in the driveway, singing from the tops of the pines, their songs trumpeting the joy of a fresh new day.

A movement in the azaleas caught his eye. He turned the scope toward it and dialed down the focus until he could make out a thick-billed, sturdy bird. He closed his eyes, heart pounding in his chest, then opened them again, sure he must be dreaming.

With its black mask and golden crown, the Barbet looked like a bird in costume for a party. The brown band across its chest that gave it its name was clearly visible. It turned and looked right at Martin, bright black eye staring into his as if it knew. *You couldn't come to me,* the bird seemed to say. *So I came to you.*

He held his breath, unbelieving, while the bird remained still, looking at him, as if waiting for an answer. He tried to stand, to move closer to the window, but pain exploded in his head, driving him to his knees. With his right hand, he groped for the windowsill, trying to pull himself up, but his arm had lost its strength. He landed hard on the floor, and lay curled into himself as the world went black.

When he woke, all was bright, the sun warm against his skin. The pain was gone, and he felt light. Light as a bird. Even as the thought came to him, he felt himself rising. Floating. The Barbet hovered beside him, beckoning. Wonder filled him as once more he was able to follow the bird into the sky. He laughed, then shouted, as he soared beside it, floating on the wind and a current of unspeakable joy.

A loud *thud* pulled Karen from sleep. At first she thought the wind from the storm had knocked something over, but as she sat and looked out the window, she saw that the rain had stopped, and the air was calm. She strained her ears, listening, but the house was quiet. Still, she couldn't shake the feeling of dread that clutched at her.

She threw back the covers and pulled on her robe, heart pounding. Telling herself she was being silly, she hurried into the hall. Dad might have fallen. If so, she'd have to wake Casey to help her get him back into bed.

She was startled to find her father's bed empty. But when she pushed the door open farther and stepped into the room, she saw his still form lying in front of the window. "Dad!" She raced to his side, and turned him onto his back. The eyes that stared up at her were empty and cold.

She sat back on her heels, a single sob escaping before she clamped her hand over her mouth. Shaking, she reached out and closed his eyes. His skin was still warm, though all the color had drained from it. She tried to find a pulse at his throat, then laid her head on his chest, praying for a heartbeat.

Only the sound of her own breathing filled her ears. She reached for Martin's hand and squeezed it. Already it was cold. She stared at his face, curiosity warring with horror. He had always been such a mystery to her. Was there anything here now to help her figure him out?

She was struck by how peaceful he looked. His expression was relaxed, the corners of his mouth tipped up, almost as if he was trying to smile. The thought was absurd. Her father wasn't a jovial man. He didn't laugh easily, and his smiles were rationed out like expensive chocolates.

But something in death had made him smile. A release from pain? Had he seen heaven at the end? A great light or an angel? Or had he learned some secret no one in this life could know?

She sat back on her heels and let the tears fall, eyes closed, shoulders shaking silently. There were so many things she'd wanted to say to him, so many things she'd wanted to hear him say. Yet at the end, they'd found something. Some…connection. A love for each other, as complicated and fraught with tension as the word was. She was grateful for that, no matter how cheated she felt about all they'd missed.

The sun shone brightly through the window by the time she pulled herself together enough to stand. She took the blanket from the bed and covered him, tucking it gently around his shoulders. When she left the room to call the funeral home, a passerby might have thought he was merely sleeping, still and peaceful.

She woke Casey and tried to break the news gently, though he shouted, "No!" and refused to believe it at first. "He was getting better," he said. "He was going to be all right."

"He was getting better. I thought so, too."

"It's not fair."

"No, it isn't."

They held each other and cried, and she thought of Tom, feeling his absence keenly. He would know the right thing to do, the right thing to say. Always, she had counted on him in a crisis.

She called Del next. He was grumpy at first, from being awakened from sleep. She suspected he'd been drinking hard the past few days, not taking Mary Elisabeth's leaving as lightly as he would have had them believe. "Del, listen," she said, breaking into his complaining. "Something happened with Dad this morning. I found him on the floor of his bedroom. He…he's gone."

"Gone? You mean dead?" He sounded awake now.

She nodded, and swallowed more tears. "Yes. I called Garrity's and they're sending someone out." They'd both gone to school with the Garrity brothers, who had taken over the operation of the funeral home from their father. "They'll be here soon if you want to come over."

"I'll be right there."

She half expected him to fall back asleep, but he was on her doorstep in twenty minutes, in khakis and a white dress shirt, his hair combed, his face freshly shaved. He spoke in solemn tones to Mike Garrity, who came with another man to transport her father's body to the funeral home. "My sister will know better what arrangements he would have wanted," Del said.

She stared at him, stunned by his willingness to give way to her judgment, as well as by his belief that she had some insight into their father's mind. "Cremation," she said after a moment. "A man who spent so much time watching birds would want his ashes scattered on the wind." She hoped that was what he'd wanted. They had never thought to discuss such an uncomfortable subject.

Casey stood in the background, sad-eyed and drooping, wilted by loss. When the hearse finally pulled out of the driveway, Del suggested they all go get some breakfast. "I'm not hungry," she said automatically.

"You need to get out of this house." He put his arm around her, his touch surprisingly gentle, and greatly comforting.

Whatever force that had been holding her together left her then, and she turned into his embrace, sobbing. He held her tightly, and patted her back. "I know," he said, over and over. "I know."

She believed him, that he *did* know the pain she felt,

that his own pain might be even deeper, since he'd never found a way to bridge the gap between himself and their difficult parent.

She raised her head and searched his face, trying to read the expression in his eyes. "He loved you," she said. "I know he did. He just didn't know how to show it."

"You believe that if you want to." He patted her shoulder again. "Did you call Mom?"

"Not yet. I thought maybe you could do that." She wasn't sure she could deal with her mother right now. Sara would no doubt try to cheer her up, but she wanted to mourn a while longer. Later, she'd appreciate her mother's efforts more.

"Sure. I can do that."

While he called their mother, Karen hugged Casey. "You okay?" she asked.

He nodded, though his face was still pale. "I'm okay." He glanced at her. "You okay?"

"Not the best shape I've ever been, but I'm hanging in there."

"We should call Dad."

"I will." But she wanted to be alone when she talked to Tom. She didn't need an audience for what could be a tense call.

"Mom says she'll be over a little later." Del joined them again.

"How did she take the news?" Karen asked.

He shrugged. "You know Mom. She doesn't let stuff like this sink in too deep."

She nodded. "I guess that's one way to cope."

"Come on. Let's at least go get some coffee," Del said. He looked back at Casey. "You, too."

She shook her head. "I need to call Tom."

"You can call him later."

"No, I need to call him now." The urgency that had engulfed her earlier returned. She need to talk to Tom. To find out what they had left between them. "You go," she said. "You and Casey."

Del raised one eyebrow, and started to say something, then shook his head. "All right. Come on, Case. Let's get the hell out of here."

When they were gone, silence cloaked the house like a heavy blanket. Karen stared at the closed door to her father's room, thinking she should go in there and clean up, but unable to face the task.

Instead, she went into her room and sat on the side of the bed, staring at the phone. Sadie followed, and sat by the bed, her chin resting on Karen's knee, eyes soft with silent support.

What would she say to Tom, after she'd got past telling him about her father's passing? He'd been so angry when he'd flown back to Denver, and she'd felt so empty. They hadn't talked since then. What did he want from her? Whatever it was, did she have it in her to give anymore?

Telling herself it was better to know the truth than to be tortured by guessing games, she picked up the receiver and dialed.

"Hello?" He sounded distracted, and she realized with a start that it was not even seven o'clock in Denver.

She wet her lips and tried to sound calm. "Tom, it's me. Karen." As if he might have forgotten the sound of her voice. "I'm sorry to wake you."

"No, that's okay. What is it? Is something wrong?"

She imagined him sitting up on the side of the bed, raking a hand through his hair and blinking, trying to come fully awake. "Why would you think something's wrong?"

"You sound funny."

Pain pinched at her heart at the concern in his voice. "It's Dad. He…he passed away early this morning." That sounded so much better than *died*. As if he'd passed on to something else. Something better, she hoped.

"I'm sorry. That's really rough."

She nodded. Her throat and jaw ached from holding back tears. "It's bad. But…he looked, I don't know…peaceful. I thought he was getting better, but there was still so much he couldn't do…." She shook her head. "Del came right over, and he was a big help."

"How's your mom?"

"Del called her. She sounded okay. A little shook up, but you know Mom. Nothing gets her down for long."

"I'll be there as soon as I can. I'll let you know as soon as I call the airlines."

"Then you'll come?"

"Of course I'll come. Unless you don't want me there."

"No, I want you here. It's just, when you left here the other day, things were so up in the air."

"We can talk about that later."

"No!" She took a deep breath, and spoke more softly. "I need to talk about it now. Before you come back here." *Before I lose my courage.*

"You're upset now. This can wait."

"No. We've waited too long already."

He sighed. The sigh of a man dealing with a stubborn child. The sound angered her. "I've been doing a lot of thinking," she said. "And I've made some decisions."

"All right. What have you decided?"

She thought of her father in the jungle, waiting on birds; and Mary Elisabeth headed to California; and Casey, who saw his future as an adventure waiting to be discovered. "Dad and I were talking the other day, and he told me that sometimes the most difficult thing is the only thing you can do. The thing your soul needs you to do. For him, that thing was birding."

"And what is that thing for you?" His voice was flat, like a stranger's.

"For me—I think it's finding a way to make our marriage work." She'd contemplated leaving. Moving out and starting over. That would be painful, but easier than staying and hashing things out. And it wasn't what her soul wanted. Something in the very kernel of her being told her she still loved Tom deeply, though she hadn't done a good job of showing him. She wanted to stay and do the work necessary to develop that feeling into something big and wonderful.

"I want that, too." The chill in his voice had vanished, and she could almost see his shoulders slumped in relief.

"There's something else, though," she said. "Something else I need."

"What is it?"

"I need to take more time for myself. I've spent so many years looking after you and the boys and the business, I've lost sight of who I really am. I have to do this if things are going to work between us."

"I want us to make them work."

"It won't be easy," she said.

"I've never been afraid of hard work."

She smiled. "That's one of the things I love about you."

"It's good to hear you say that."

"I've been practicing." She held the phone with both hands, wishing she were holding him instead. That plane from Denver couldn't get here fast enough. "If I keep this up, I might actually get good at all this emotional stuff."

"I never meant to hurt you," he said. "I just

felt...desperate. Like nothing I could do would get through to you how much I need you."

"I know." She sniffed and swiped tears from her eyes. "When I do get home, let's plan a trip somewhere, just the two of us. We need to spend some time together away from the business and the boys and everything else that gets in the way of just being together."

"That sounds like a great idea."

She cleared her throat, heart racing again at the thought of what she was about to propose. "And I want to take some time just for me, too. Time when I don't have to be the boys' mother or the office manager or any of those other roles. I need to spend some time finding out who I really am, down inside."

"Do you have anything in particular in mind?"

"I was thinking...maybe a bird-watching trip. I know it's a little crazy, but I've taken it up since I've been here and, well, all that time sitting outside, being still and looking at nature—it's very soothing. It gives me time to listen to the thoughts in my head, instead of drowning them out with all the to-do lists I'm used to keeping in there."

"All right. That sounds fair. I was thinking, too— there's a counselor in the next building over. Maybe it wouldn't hurt to talk to her. I mean, we might need some help if we're really going to do things differently."

"Yeah. That's a good idea." She sagged onto the bed, relief leaving her weak in the knees. That her stand-on-his-own-two-feet husband was willing to accept outside help told her how serious he was about fixing their problems.

"We can do this," he said.

"We can." She smiled into the phone. If she was going to start doing things differently, now was as good a time as any to begin. "Tom?"

"Yes?"

"I love you. I really do." That wasn't so hard. With practice, the words would probably roll off her tongue. But she would never take them for granted. Fate was still out there listening, and she had too much to lose if she screwed things up this time.

After she'd hung up the phone, she wandered out onto the front porch, Sadie at her heels. She wanted to escape the house for at least a little while. Pinecones and broken branches littered the front yard, which glistened wetly in the sunlight. Birdsong lent a tropical feel to the setting. She picked up her father's binoculars from the table by the spot where she'd often settled his wheelchair. He would spend hours here, scanning the treetops, never tiring of studying the behavior and habits of the birds.

The binoculars were old, heavy metal with the black paint worn through to silver where his fingers had gripped them so many hours. She fit her fingers over these worn places, and it was as if he was there with her, the way he was when she was small. He'd hold his hands over hers and show her how to bring the glasses to her eyes and adjust the focus.

A sharp cry, almost human, startled her, and she almost dropped the glasses. When she turned toward the sound, she found a crow, perched in the azalea bush beside the porch. It stared at her with one bright, intelligent eye, head tilted to one side, studying her. She held her breath, fascinated, until it spread its wings and jumped into the air. She watched it soar higher and higher.

She raised the glasses and followed it over the tops of the tall pines, feeling her own spirits lift. It was as if her father had given her one last gift—this assurance that she, too, would find what she needed to be whole. That she would discover her own way to soar.

There comes a time in every woman's life when she needs more.

Sometimes finding what you want means leaving everything you love. Big-hearted, warm and funny, Flying Lessons is a story of love and courage as Beth Holt Martin sets out to change her life and her marriage, for better or for worse.

Flying Lessons

by

Peggy Webb

HARLEQUIN®

HN42 Available May 2006
TheNextNovel.com

Next

REQUEST YOUR FREE BOOKS!

You're never too old to sneak out at night

BJ thinks her younger sister, Iris, needs a love interest. So she does what any mature woman would do and organizes an Over-Fifty Singles Night. When her matchmaking backfires it turns out to be the best thing either of them could have hoped for.

Over 50's Singles Night

by Ellyn Bache

HARLEQUIN
Next

Available April 2006
TheNextNovel.com

HN37

A Boca Babe
on a Harley?

Harriet's former life as a Boca Babe—where only
looks, money and a husband count—left her
struggling for freedom. Finally gaining control
of her path, she's leaving that life behind as she
takes off on her Harley. When she drives straight
into a mystery that is connected to her past, will
she be able to stay true to her future?

Dirty Harriet
by Miriam Auerbach

HN40
Available April 2006
TheNextNovel.com

Life is full of hope.

Facing a family crisis, Melinda and
her husband are forced to look
at their lives and end up learning
what is really important.

Falling Out
of Bed

by
Mary Schramski

Available May 2006
TheNextNovel.com

HARLEQUIN®
Next™

It's a dating jungle out there!

Four thirtysomething women with a fear of dating form a network of support to empower each other as they face the trials and travails of modern matchmaking in Los Angeles.

The I Hate To Date Club

by
Elda Minger

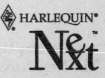

HN43

Available May 2006
TheNextNovel.com